ORIOLE PARK BRANCH

### DATE DUE    07/03

| | | |
|---|---|---|
| DEC 0 2 2003 | | |
| AUG 1 7 2004 | | |
| | | |
| | | |
| | | |
| | | |
| | | |
| | | |
| | | |
| | | |
| | | |
| | | |
| | | |
| | | |
| | | |
| | | |
| | | |

DEMCO 38-296

# Outlaw Tamer.

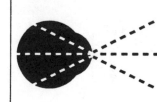

# Outlaw Tamer.

## Max Brand

**Thorndike Press • Thorndike, Maine**

Thorndike Large Print ® Western Series edition published in 1993 by arrangement with Golden West Literary Agency.

The tree indicium is a trademark of Thorndike Press.

This book is printed on acid-free, high opacity paper. ⊚

Set in 16 pt. News Plantin by Minnie B. Raven.

---

**Library of Congress Cataloging in Publication Data**

Brand, Max, 1892–1944
    Outlaw tamer / Max Brand.
      p.  cm.
    ISBN 1-56054-706-5 (alk. paper : lg. print)
    1. Large type books.  I. Title.
    [PS3511.A8708  1993]
    813'.52—dc20                › 93-8986
                                            CIP

# Outlaw Tamer

# 1

Of course, a forced sale is always a painful thing. Dunstan felt wicked about it; partly because he knew that he had bought in the Morgan place for about thirty per cent of its real value, and partly because he knew that Morgan had not deserved to lose. That is, he knew in his heart that bad luck had beaten the doctor more than anything else. That was the very reason that Peter Dunstan put on his grimmest face; and for the ride to the Morgan place that morning, he selected the toughest and the meanest horse in his string.

He had a good string of horses, all with high strains of breeding, but that good blood was crossed with common, old mustang stock. Peter Dunstan liked horses of that ilk — fine-standing fellows with a good deal of the devil tucked away in their hearts.

This morning, he had a black-legged gray beneath his saddle. The gelding fought him for a full ten minutes before he would straighten out and take the road. Peter Dunstan let him go like the wind, then, and Dunstan's men followed in the rear.

They were accustomed to following their master at some distance. Not that they were men who would willingly take the dust of another. Indeed, Peter Dunstan had handpicked them for just the opposite reason. All his hands were selected because they knew horses, and knew cattle, and understood that a horse exists only to be ridden; that a cow exists only to be turned into so many pounds of beef. Besides this, each was a good fighting man. With knife, gun, or fist, there was not a man in the group, from the little red-headed man who rode aslant, to the big solidly seated fellow with black hair, who could not hold his own and more ninety-nine out of a hundred times.

If there were long hours and poor feed on the Dunstan Ranch, it was a consolation to know that the boss had long hours and poor feed, himself. If every man there had had cause to understand that Dunstan, in spite of his forty-five years, was his master — whether with fist or with gun — there was a deeper satisfaction in the knowledge that Peter Dunstan would fight *for* them even more readily than he would fight with them.

Mr. Dunstan had not chosen the gray gelding in vain. The nervous, powerful brute had plunged and shied and bucked all the way across the dusty hills. His rider was in a fighting humor when he arrived at his destination

— just the sort of a humor that he needed to face the doctor. Yet, when he encountered Dr. Henry Morgan, he saw that he had built up a savage spirit in vain.

The doctor did not intend to make any faces over the affair. He had played a big game in this effort to dry farm so much territory. He had lost a great amount of money and time. Yet, after his failure, he would not whine. He met the man who had paid him three dollars in cash for ten dollars in value with a smile.

"Now, Mr. Dunstan," said he, "I'll take you into my office and show you my plans. I'm glad that you came early. I had hoped that you would be over yesterday, but there is still time before I have to ride for the train. Before I go, I can put you in mind of everything that I wanted to do, here in the valley."

"You mean," said Peter Dunstan, "in farming?"

"I mean that, of course."

"Why, then," said the rancher, "I'll tell you how it is. I've got a lot of respect for you, Dr. Morgan, but for the thing that you've been trying to do out here I have to tell you bluntly that I don't give a hang!"

He thrust out his square jaw. He would much prefer to make a fight out of the transaction. The doctor merely sighed and shook his head with a smile.

"I was afraid that it would be that way," said he. "I had hoped that the man who took over this place would inherit my own ambitions with it. But I see that that cannot be, and the plows and the harrows and the rest must go to rust."

Dunstan grunted, and his swift eye ran over the farmhouse. That active eye of his instantly stripped away these unessentials, and already, in spirit, he saw the dust clouds arising at the very foot of the walls of the house. He saw the hitching rack where the ponies of his cowpunchers should be tethered conveniently beside the door. It would not take long for their sharp hoofs to trample the neglected lawn to powder!

Perhaps Dr. Morgan saw something of this in the hawklike gaze of his companion. He said:

"Well, at least you'll be interested in the hay press. You need winter feed, Dunstan."

"Aye, there's sense to that. Come along then, Morgan, if you will, and show me the press. Though I suppose that I could find out about it for myself."

The doctor pointed to a small corral which they were passing.

"There's a prize winner," said he. "That big Durham bull has a pedigree that a duke could envy. The list is longer than my arm."

"But why the corral?" asked the rancher.

"Oh, he needs hand tending and hand feeding, and all the rest. Grooming is as important to him as it is to feed him, almost."

"Bah!" exclaimed Peter Dunstan. "Where do you find men who'll do that sort of work? My boys would never lay a curry comb on the back of a bull. But they might dress him down with a quirt. Eh, boys?"

The subdued laughter of the Dunstan hands was like the looming of distant thunder.

"Whip him out," said the rancher, "and let him take care of himself in the open, will you?"

"Man, man!" cried the doctor. "You don't mean that! He'll be horned to death by the first wild devil of a bull that he meets on your range."

Mr. Dunstan turned toward the other a grave face with speaking eyes. He was not accustomed to hearing his orders questioned in the presence of his hands. He waved them on to execute his orders, saying to the doctor:

"He'll learn to care and fend for himself, or else he'll die. That's the way that I have with my men, and that's the way that I have with cow and horse. I find that it prospers the breed in the long run."

The doctor shook his head. "He's not meant

11

for it," said he. "He's not trained for it! A ton of fat and good nature! Look at his sleepy eyes! He doesn't need that ring through his nose. I could lead him about with my bare hand — I've done it!"

"But perhaps," said the rancher, "when he has to work for himself, that ton of fat and bone will turn into a ton of bone and muscle. Perhaps he'll wake up. Do I want sleeping blood like that in my calves? No, sir, I want the heart of fire. That makes the stuff that will not have to be corralled and fed all through the winter. Look at the fat fool! He won't leave even when the bars are down! Whip him out, punchers!"

They whipped him out, readily enough. With their quirts cracking and cutting at his rump, he was sent lumbering over the next hill and away toward the open. The doctor watched him go with a dying dream in his eyes. The ribbons which that bull had won were delights which had haunted his sleep for many a night. He said nothing, and led the way on toward the hay press.

It stood in a hollow beside the butt end of a great stack of hay. A hundred-and-fifty-ton stack that monster pile had once been, and still in what remained standing there were forty solid tons of fine feed. Beside the loose hay stood the neatly squared and growing stack of the bales, flaring in the bright sun like cubes of pale, polished amber.

They could distinguish these things, but not the minute details, for the whole scene was obscured with a mist of dust, ever rising as the fork dragged fresh sections of the stack toward the feeding platform, as the fork horse plodded out or sluggishly backed, or where the beater rose and fell in the box, or most of all where the four power horses trotted in their jerky circle.

"Bale!" shouted the power driver.

The bale roller leaped for the doghouse under the feed platform. He snatched his bar and jammed open the heavy door; as it swung wide he caught at the wire heads which the wire-puncher shoved through from the farther side of the box.

"A good bale roller," said the doctor, "ought to take the wire off the last hook — he ought to be waiting for it — you see?"

Sure enough, the bale roller had gripped the last wire the instant the wire-puncher's needle slid through. The wire was tied with a single twisting grip of the gloved left hand.

"Tied!" yelled the bale roller.

He caught his hook from the nail above his head and sank it in the top of the bale as the power team lurched ahead, and the heavy beater rose. He jerked the bale out, turned and "broke" it across his knee — all with his right hand. With his left, he slammed the door shut, disengaged the hook, and with it pulled home the locking bar — all of this before the beater could rise a scant few feet, and the feeder push down the first slug of the new bale.

"Aye," said the rancher, "all very good. But where d'you get the men that will do this sort of dog's work?"

"From dawn to dark," said the doctor, "but they get as high as seven dollars a day for it."

"You could pay my men," said the rancher, "seven dollars an hour, but they wouldn't make themselves slaves for that. Slaves to a master, or slaves to money, what difference does it make? The fellows in my outfit want to be free men!"

He said this a little louder than he had spoken before, because there was no reason why his men should not hear the noble sentiment which he had just spoken in their behalf. They did hear, as they nodded, self-satisfied.

"Aye," said Peter Dunstan, "and now I can see the sort of men that have to be hired for this work. Dead men — sleeping men — like the fat bull that you kept in the corral, Morgan! Look yonder! It makes me yawn."

"Why," said the doctor, "he seems a very

well set-up fellow."

"What does the body count!" cried Dunstan. "It's the heart of fire, man — the heart of fire. It isn't the show horse that wins the race. It's the broken-kneed cripple, perhaps, if he has wings in his mind and a heart of fire. And that poor devil yonder — why, he doesn't live, he sleeps! There's more life in the eye of a dead fish than in his eye!"

"I am sorry you think that!" said Dr. Morgan. "Because I want to talk to you about that very boy. You remember that I said I should ask you to keep one of my men?"

"It was written into the bill of sale," said the rancher. "But I hope, Morgan, that you won't wish on me a joke like that — a dead lump like that!"

"I'm sorry," said Morgan, "but that's the very man!"

# 2

At this, the rancher shrugged his shoulders ever so slightly, as one who said: "This burden shall not gall me very long."

It seemed that the doctor read his mind, for he added: "I shall want to ask you to give me your word on it, my friend."

Here Dunstan rebelled. He was not the most scrupulous man in the world, though more so than many gave him credit for being. It could truly be said that he was one whose naked word was a more strongly binding power than another man's bond.

"Now," he said in resistance, "look here, Morgan, you know me and you know my men — because you've lived in the same county with us for quite a spell. But still you don't know us well enough, or you would never want to send a man like that along with us. Or is he only a boy, Morgan?"

He said this hopefully.

"I don't know," said Morgan. "Sometimes I think that he's a case of arrested development, and that some day he'll take the next step and really grow up. Then again, I'm forced to feel that he's just simple. He's twenty-three, Dunstan."

"Twenty-three!" said Dunstan with a groan. "And still leading a power horse up and down along one track all the day long! What a job for a grown man! Why, I was running a ranch at that age — you had a degree — we were our full selves, except for the lines in our faces and the toughness in our heads. Here's a man of that age just leading a horse up and down all the day long!"

"I'll freely admit that it's bad, and very, very bad," said Morgan. "But there's a story behind this affair. You must understand that this lad's mother and father both worked for my family most of their lives. Long before I came West, when the mother died, she begged me to take care of the boy. Now, Dunstan, I'd be glad to take him back to the city with me, since I've lost my hold on the country, but I really believe that his one chance for getting back to normal is in the country. In the city, he sits like a block of wood all the day long. Nothing interests him. But in the country he *has* interests. Queer ones — mostly animals. Shall I tell you about him?"

"If I've got to have him," said the rancher darkly, "and if I've got to keep him rolled up in cotton batting and out of the way of harm among my fighting men, you'd better tell me everything that you can."

"He spent most of his life in the city, as I was telling you — just stolid — only waking up for flashes. I tried to have him taught reading and writing, for instance. I was interested in the case. I got in an expert. And the expert teacher and psychologist worked like mad for three months. Well, the boy learned nothing — nothing, Dunstan, and to this day he can barely read or write."

Dunstan threw up his hands.

"It's a good deal to wish on a man," said he. "Can he feed himself?"

"Oh, aye. He can do that and more."

"He'll work, at least," said the rancher, "and I may be able to find some fool job like turning the handle of a grindstone for him to do all day long."

"He'd never do it," said the doctor. "Oh, he'd never do that! He was three years here on the farm before he found work that he would do."

"In fact," said Dunstan in irritation, "you're turning over to me a plain case of charity!"

The doctor was a mild man, as has been pointed out. But he was not a man without spirit, and now he answered: "No, Dunstan. I'm not a fool. I would never do that."

It was said in such a tone that the rancher felt as if a whip had fallen upon him; but not a lash which he could resent, because it had fallen upon his heart only.

"Very well," said he, "then I'm to keep a hay press running, so that this fellow can have a job like this to his liking? But go on, Morgan, and tell me all about the idiot!"

The last word made the doctor wince in turn, but he continued gravely: "Very well. The teacher, as I told you, gave up in despair. He said that Sandy was not a fool, but simply asleep above the eyes, if you know what I mean by that."

"I suppose I do. After looking at his eyes, I suppose that I *do* understand what you mean."

"I got the boy here to the West with me, and he's developed a great deal in the past dozen years, since I have been here. So that I can tell you that he will not be a case of charity for you. He cannot do many things well, but he has a talent for handling certain animals. If there's a need of any hard shooting which you and your men can't manage to handle, you can turn the job over to Sandy. He'll turn the trick for you."

For all the apparent carelessness of the doctor, he had put his heel upon a very tender spot in Dunstan's honor, and he knew it.

"As for the hard shooting," said Dunstan, "I suppose that if there is anything that I can't handle, one of my men will be able to do it."

The doctor answered calmly: "Isn't there a cattle-killing grizzly that has been living on your cows for two or three years — and always on your own range, man? Are you leaving her there for fun, or is it because you *want* her to stay?"

Mr. Peter Dunstan grew hot in the face.

"You are meaning, that the idiot could bag the old devil who's been eating my cows?"

"I mean that."

"I have a thousand dollars," said Dunstan, "that say you are wrong!"

"My friend," said the doctor, "I bet now and then, but never on a sure thing. If you send the boy after the bear, he'll get it. You take my word for it."

Mr. Dunstan was very loath to do so. There were a great many questions which he wished to ask, but he refrained, because there was something in the face of the doctor that said plainly that he meant what he had said.

"Very well," said the rancher, "if he can turn that trick for me, I'll admit that he has earned his board for a year or two. What else can he do, my friend?"

"If you have some bad-acting horseflesh on your ranch — and I believe that you like them that way — he *may* be able to tame the outlaws. If he takes a fancy to them, I mean."

"*If* he takes a fancy to them? He'll never take a fancy to any of the bad actors up my way," declared Dunstan.

"That's to be found out. I'll tell you this: I took him to town with me to see a circus, and in the circus, one feature was a wild horse with a standing offer of a hundred dollars to any puncher who could stay on its back for five minutes. In this section of the country, you know there are plenty of the boys to take up a bet like that and call it easy money if they get off with sound bones. That horse was a devil, however. It tossed those punchers as fast as they could get into the saddle. Big Sandy, yonder, was delighted — not with the riding, but with the meanness of that horse.

"He begged me to buy the brute, and when I asked him why, he said that he would soon tame it. I bought the horse and brought it on the farm at the end of three lassoes and with hobbles on its legs.

"When I got it out here, I turned it over to Sandy. He had it put in a big corral by itself; then he started to work on it. How, I never could tell, unless it were by fascination. It was about two weeks before he led that horse up to the front door by the *mane!*"

"The devil!" cried the startled Dunstan.

"The day after that, he was riding the horse across the fields, sitting bareback on it. I saw that the youngster had power over horses, after that. When the bad horse fell and broke two of its legs, I thought that Sandy would die of grief. He would actually go to sit and mourn at the spot where it had been shot. I finally offered him another horse to take its place, but he wouldn't listen to me until Cristobal Mendez came by with a roan demon of a mare —"

"I saw that man-eater," said the rancher, nodding.

"When Sandy saw that mare, he took a great fancy to her, and begged me to buy her. I remembered what he had done before, and I got her from Mendez for ten dollars. He was tired of venturing his head behind her heels."

"The devil!" muttered Dunstan. "Did he actually do anything with that wild mare?"

"Look at the fork horse again," said the doctor, grinning.

The rancher looked; behold! The animal which big Sandy led up and down through the dust was a sleek roan mare!

The curiosity of Peter Dunstan was like the curiosity of a lion, in so much that where his eye traveled, his paw was apt to strike. Now that he had decided that this youth was worthy of more investigation, he touched his gelding with the spur and, at a bound, it placed him beside young Sandy Sweyn. The roan mare was at that moment in the act of advancing, and dragging the fork with its little load of hay out of the stack.

Dunstan's fullest attention was riveted upon the mare and the long, light, swinging stride with which she walked away under the burden.

He saw the fork tripped — the load of hay dropped with a jar upon the feed table, and Sandy Sweyn commenced to back up the roan.

It was a different matter from her forward progress. She had pricked her ears willingly enough, as though she did not at all mind the struggle of the lift. To back up — that was a thing that went against her grain.

Back went the short, sharp ears, with a quiver of malice and hatred. She shook her head, and she switched her tail nervously. Peter Dunstan began to feel anxious. Assuredly, had he stood in that place behind the famous heels of that man-killer, he would have jumped for safety. Not so the half-wit. He simply jerked impatiently at the singletree. He said not a word. It did not even occur to him, apparently, to touch the reins which were festooned about his neck, but he strained back upon the singletree in silence.

Peter Dunstan observed two things: The first was a great shock of surprise to him —

for the roan mare, after a brief instant of hesitation, did indeed begin to back up, obedient to that pressure — not with the lounging, sloppy step of a work horse, but a neat, precise, high leg action. She backed as straight as a string, and as fast and light as the forker could gather in the spare length of rope before he dragged the fork back upon the stack.

This was all very strange to Mr. Peter Dunstan. For it was affording, in the most simple manner, the surest proof that the half-wit had fully conquered the great mare. Yet this was not the most remarkable matter which the rancher had observed.

For the sleeves of Sandy Sweyn were no longer than his brown elbows. When he pulled back upon the singletree, Mr. Dunstan had observed that upon the forearm of the fork horse driver an intricate tangle of twisting muscles leaped into view. Now Sandy Sweyn leaned dreamily against the side of the mare; she leaned a little against him, and the relaxed arm of Sandy Sweyn looked not merely large, but soft and round with fat.

Peter Dunstan had seen, and he knew that it was not fat at all. By the forearm you will tell the man. It was not the mere bulk and the sinewy development of that forearm which interested the rancher; it was even more the taper formation, which suggested an incredible strength of upper arm and shoulder and back.

There was only some five feet and eleven inches of Sandy Sweyn, but the rancher on his second guess shrewdly suspected that he carried well over two hundred pounds of muscle. A burden, in fact, which needed the mighty frame of such a horse as the roan to carry him fast and far.

Peter Dunstan rode closer and he looked down at Sandy's hand. It was as he had suspected. That hand was not squared and blunted by much labor; it was as tapered and graceful as the hand of any gentleman of leisure who has never gripped a heavier tool than a golf club. No, that miracle of strength which had been revealed to Mr. Dunstan upon the arm of Sandy Sweyn was not the power which is the result of honest labor, long performed. It was a mere gift of nature.

A sudden anger burned in the heart of Dunstan. Ah, how cruelly unlucky it was that this simple creature should have been endowed with the might of a Hercules, a power to which even the stout and famous right arm of Peter Dunstan was like the power of a child; that this boy should have been endowed with the singular ability to rule even such a dreadful malefactor as the roan mare, Cleo. And then to blur and spoil the splendid picture, that he should be — a half-wit!

Then he lost all conscience. It was not right that to this stronghanded idiot such a treasure as the glorious mare should be intrusted. It was not right by any means! She was fitted to bear upon her back a ruler of men — such a one as Peter Dunstan himself, and his two hundred pounds of fighting strength. Peter decided to take her from Sandy Sweyn — not by force. He would not be guilty of such an act — but by deception.

"Sandy," said he, "what will you take for the roan?"

Sandy Sweyn looked up to him out of vague eyes. They were a strange color, and they gave the strangeness to the face of the youth, Peter Dunstan decided. For the rest, he was a handsome fellow, though, perhaps, his features were a little too heavily and grossly made. The hair of Sandy Sweyn was tawny in hue, and the eyes of Sandy Sweyn were tawny, also — the color of a lion's mane. Such a color in eyes Peter Dunstan had never seen before except in the dazzled eye of an owl.

He waited a long moment for an answer, but when it came it shocked him.

"I don't know," said Sandy Sweyn, "but I suppose that I'd take a faster horse for the roan — if I can get one."

"Ah!" said Peter Dunstan, "you don't really

love the mare, then?"

"I like her pretty well," said Sandy Sweyn, and he ran his mighty fingers through the mane of Cleo, "but I would like a faster horse better!"

# 3

As Mr. Dunstan felt that he would be able to close the bargain, he felt an eye upon him. When he looked up, he saw that it was the doctor, studying him with greatest attention. Peter Dunstan flinched, as though he had been caught in the commission of a most unworthy act.

He rode back to Dr. Morgan.

"Of all the half-wits that I've ever seen," said he, "this fellow is the queerest."

"Perhaps," said Dr. Morgan, "he is. But for my part, I've never been able to make up my mind as to whether he's the half-wit — or whether he has the real sense, and I'm the fool."

"I'd like to know what you mean by that!" said Dunstan.

"Why," replied the doctor, "it's really hard for me to explain, except in a general way. But you have heard a good deal of talk, now and then, about the primitive man — the abysmal brutes?"

"Oh," said the rancher, "I see what you mean. Well, I suppose that you may be right, in a way. I am able to imagine that the cave dwellers may have been like that fellow. He's born just a thousand years or so after his time — or maybe a million years, doctor."

The doctor nodded.

"That's one way of looking at it," said he. "That's the idea that got into my head after I had known him only a few years. But lately I've been considering the other side of the question — the opposite side."

"What do you mean by that?"

"That he may have been born about a million years *ahead* of his time."

The rancher started in the saddle. "You mean, that the human race will go backward toward the brute type again?"

"No, I'm an optimist. I think that we'll always slowly advance — until the human race freezes to death — unless it has found a way of transplanting itself to some warmer planet by that time. But I wonder if this Sandy Sweyn isn't a type of what we are going to be as we climb the ladder?"

The rancher struck one hand heavily into the other.

"Now, look here, old-timer," said he. "I'm a simple fellow, and I don't pretend to know a lot of things that are just A B C to you. But I hate to fool around with stuff that may be nonsense. Are you calling this half-wit a step toward a perfect man?"

"I don't want to be mysterious," said the doctor, "but, frankly, I'm talking about an idea that only is half out of the shadow in my own mind. I mean — this fellow who appears like a half-wit to us might be a most tremendous person if he ever were to have a chance to develop himself. Well, how is a man developed? How did you and I get our education? By playing and talking with other boys of our own age, and so growing up to have what we call good sense. This Sandy Sweyn has never found people of his own kind."

"Because, of course," said the rancher, "most of his kind are sent to institutions where they're not apt to do themselves any harm."

"Do you think that?" said the doctor. "Ah, well. Perhaps you are right. But the other idea sticks in my crop. That boy needs conversation which you and I and other people can't give him. He's a mute because there is no one to understand him — except animals!"

"Confound it, Morgan, that is too much, unless you intend it as a joke."

"Wait till you have a better chance to know him. You'll see what a considerable distance he is from being a fool."

"Aye," said the rancher, "I'm going to study

30

him. But first of all I want to buy that mare of his."

"He won't sell her."

"Why, man, that shows that you really don't know him. He has said already that he'll give her up for a faster horse, if I can find one for him."

There was triumph in the tone of the rancher. The doctor flushed a little. As a matter of fact, he had expended a great deal of patience and self-control upon the rancher. Now he was near the end of his string. He answered calmly:

"I'd like to wager that you won't find a horse very soon to beat Cleo."

"Nonsense!" answered Peter Dunstan. "She's a fine brute, but too heavy to move fast. I have a dozen ponies who could step right past her."

"Do you think so? Well, Dunstan, I'll bet you that you haven't a single *one* that can outrun her."

It was the time for Dunstan to flush — and he turned a dark and dangerous red.

"Do you mean to say, Dr. Morgan, that you think this gelding I'm on couldn't walk away from the mare?"

"I mean just that."

"You'd bet on it?"

"I shall be breaking my rule if I do, for

I never bet on a sure thing."

"A sure thing, doctor," said he sarcastically, "is the sort of a matter that a fellow will put *real* money on."

"Dunstan, I don't like to rob you."

Peter Dunstan broke out with a huge oath.

"Man, man," he cried, "if you're fool enough to back the roan against this flyer, I have five hundred dollars to say that I'll win."

"Do you mean that?" asked the doctor stiffly.

"As the boys used to say — put up or shut up!"

"Dunstan," said the doctor, turning pale with anger, "I'll tell you that I have seen the mare run, and therefore I have an advantage over you."

"Bah!" said Dunstan, "I've heard the stories about her when she was running wild. But I tell you, man, that she weighs close to thirteen hundred pounds — or even more. No brute of that tonnage can really move with a horse like the one under my saddle. When a wild horse is chased, there's no rider, no saddle, no cinches, no bridle and bit to bother it. That's why the mare baffled the hunters for so long. Besides, she's a tricky fiend. You can see that in her eye, quickly enough. Don't tell me, Morgan, that she could move in the same flight with the running type."

The doctor exclaimed: "I tell you that mare will walk away from your gelding. And if you want to bet on it, make it five hundred or five thousand. I don't care which. Five thousand would teach you a lesson."

That talk was just a shade franker than any that the rancher had listened to since he became a known man in the West. His fighting jaw thrust out ominously.

"Do you mean that you would put up five thousand dollars on the race, doctor?"

"My checkbook is in my pocket. Shall I write my check?"

Mr. Dunstan answered: "I'd just as soon tell you that I'm carrying *my* checkbook, also. If you don't mind, we'll leave the checks with one of the boys as stakeholder —"

In another moment two brown hands were scratching away at narrow, colored strips of paper. Then the two checks were in the hand of "Shorty." His blue eyes blazed when he heard the terms of the bet. He asked with an almost moaning eagerness whether there were any other people on the Morgan place who would back the roan with hard cash.

Oh, yes, there were plenty. All the crew of the hay press, said the doctor, would be willing to bet their shirts on her ability to beat the gelding thoroughly. The doctor was right. The instant that the rumor of the race reached the hay-press crew, the baling operations stopped at once, and the crew swarmed out to make sure that the race was indeed to take place.

All was not ready, however, when the doctor and the rancher had decided upon the contest. There still remained another party to the contract. At first he seemed to raise insuperable difficulties. That was Sandy Sweyn.

He had fallen to work, the instant that the hay press stopped in its operations. With a hard-twisted wisp of hay he was rubbing down the roan assiduously. As the living dust cloud in which she had been walking cleared away, her coat could be seen to glimmer and then to shine like a burnished metal under the swift and powerful strokes of Sandy.

The rancher, observing her anew, felt a sudden sinking of the heart. He was aware, for the first time, of the reach of her legs, of the great bone with which they were finished off beneath knee and hock. Still, such was the massive bulk of haunch and shoulder that he was encouraged again almost at once. Looking at her up to the belly, with its clean line like the hull of a racing yacht, she appeared a true flyer.

Above that point, she might almost have been a workhorse. No, not quite so bad as that, for no workhorse since the beginning of time ever had muscles so neatly outlined and so sleek. Such bulk and suggested speed combined had never been seen by the comprehending eye of Mr. Dunstan, unless it were in the single glimpse he had had of the naked forearm of Sandy Sweyn, when the latter had tugged at the singletree of the mare.

The doctor explained to the youth with care that he wished to have him ride the mare against the rancher's gelding. Sandy Sweyn listened, his eyes fixed not upon the doctor but upon the gelding with the strange blank look which filled the rancher already with horror and wonder and aversion.

"I dunno," said Sandy Sweyn, "but I guess that I ain't gunna ride Cleo against a lame hoss!"

The rancher stared, then shouted: "Lame horse? Lame nonsense! Doctor, you can't back out of the bet like this! The checks are posted, and I intend to collect. It will be a sound lesson to you. Stick to medicine and to dry farming, doctor, but don't risk your valuable opinion on horseflesh, after this, and prepare to back it up with so much hard cash!"

That was not a very rude speech, according to Peter Dunstan's standards of harsh and kind. Yet it made the doctor flush and toss his head, like a colt when the spur pricks, and it is conscious of no fault.

"It's not *my* remark," said the doctor. "It's Sandy Sweyn that says that."

"What the devil does he know about this horse, when he sees it for the first time?"

"He's never wrong, Dunstan. I assure you that he knows what he's speaking about, or else he doesn't speak!"

Peter Dunstan, with the flaring vision of five thousand dollars at hand, could not restrain himself. It would be a stroke that would fatten his bank account on the one hand and give him a bit of excellent table talk the rest of his days, on the other. For both reasons the prospect was prized by Peter Dunstan.

He said, at last: "Look here, man, and see whether or not this is a crippled horse!"

He whirled the gelding away, raced it a few strides, and then swept it back again.

"Did it limp? Did it falter?" shouted Peter Dunstan hotly, from his cloud of dust.

Then he was aware of Sandy Sweyn approaching, with the unhitched roan mare following like a dog at his heels.

"He ain't gunna show up lame until he's rode hard and begins to bang the ground racing," said Sandy Sweyn. "This here is where he's gunna break down."

Raising his blank eyes to the face of the rancher, he pressed his forefinger deep into the muscular shoulder of the gelding. Beneath

36

him, Mr. Dunstan felt a shudder of pain go through the body of the fine horse.

He glanced sharply down and into the dull eyes of the youth, trying to find his soul and perhaps a hidden cunning there. All he found was an impenetrable wall of mist.

"I'll try him again," said Peter Dunstan. "I've ridden long enough to be able to tell a lame horse about as well as the next one."

He carried the gelding off again in a brisk canter. However, the action of the rangy creature seemed perfection to him, and to all of them who stood by and watched, as well. Peter Dunstan came back more fixed in his purpose than ever.

"My horse is ready, man!" he called to the doctor, as he swung to the ground. "I've posted my forfeit and I've offered my horse. Now what will you do next?"

There was a clamor of noise around them where the hay balers were laying their bets with the punchers of Dunstan's train. Big bets for them — thirty — fifty — a hundred dollars — according as a man had been unlucky and had to post his pay of the month to come, or as he had been more successful in his recent adventure at poker. In the midst of this confusion, Sandy Sweyn calmly protested that he would not race the mare against a lame horse.

"But," said the doctor, "he *wants* to risk the gelding."

"Has he asked his hoss whether or not it wants to run?" asked Sandy Sweyn. "No, he ain't. Because you can see in the eye of that hoss that he don't feel fast to-day!"

Peter Dunstan, leaving the gelding behind him, strode straight up to the half-wit and pointed a finger sternly in his face.

"Look here," said he. "We've heard enough nonsense from you, Sandy. Now we're going to have this race run, and you're going to ride in it whether you want to or not. D'you hear me? Because from this time on, *I'm* your boss, Sandy. And you come to me for orders!"

Sandy Sweyn looked in amazement from the tall form of the angry rancher to the saddened face of the doctor.

"You know," explained Dr. Morgan gently, "that I have to leave this place, Sandy. And you wouldn't be happy in the city where I am going to live. You couldn't take Cleo along with you, you know."

A dark understanding broke upon the face of Sandy.

"I couldn't take Cleo?"

"No."

"Then I'd have to stay here, I suppose," said Sandy Sweyn. "But is *he* going to be my boss, then?"

He pointed dubiously at Peter Dunstan.

"He owns this place, Sandy. And you like the place, don't you? You like the place and you know it. The people here understand you, and you understand them. So I thought it would be better for you to stay on here with Mr. Dunstan. He will take care of you."

"Ah," said Sandy, sighing and looking with his blank eyes upon the rancher, "it don't seem to me like there is much but trouble lyin' ahead."

Then he turned to the mare and began to strip the harness from her back.

A saddle was quickly fitted to her. In the meantime, Mr. Dunstan was equally busy. If the roan had been performing brutally hard work in the dust beside the haystack, the gelding had just had a hard canter across the country, and Mr. Dunstan did not believe in throwing away any chances. It was not his style; for life is life, and money is money. Why should one be careless with it?

Straightway, he said to Shorty, the lightest in body and the toughest in soul of all who rode in his train:

"Shorty, can you handle the big boy today?"

Shorty looked askance at the tall form of his master's horse.

"I'll handle him or kill him," said the genial

Shorty. "You leave him to me! Just shorten them stirrups a bit, will you?"

"I'll do that," said Dunstan, delighted, "and if you can ride him, Shorty, as I know you can, you get — an extra fifty, if you win."

For Mr. Dunstan was not needlessly generous. There is no law that compels a man to make large offers, you know. However, the mere honor of the task was enough to persuade Shorty; he tingled with pride to the roots of his very red hair as he strode with a swagger through his hardy companions.

"You soft-shelled suckers," said the amiable Shorty, "leave me be and gimme room."

They hardly begrudged him this speech — they were so entirely rejoiced to see a hundred and fifty pounds in the saddle on the gelding, instead of the two hundred at which Mr. Peter Dunstan turned the beam.

The doctor, however, was amazed.

"Why," said he, "I thought you were to do the riding yourself, man!"

"Did you think that? Was there anything said about riders? Why, you can pick out any lightweight that you please, doctor. And then double the bets, if you wish!"

The right fist of the doctor doubled into an iron-hard knot, but he did not strike. Whether with hand or weapon, he knew that to engage with this bully would be simply to invite humiliation.

"The course then, Dunstan?" said he tersely.

"Around that black rock and back again, d'you think?"

The doctor allowed himself to smile.

"That's nearly a mile and a half, man," said he, "and distance tells in favor of the lightly-weighted horse, of course. Do you seriously suggest it, Dunstan? With seventy pounds less in the saddle than goes on Cleo?"

The nerve of the rancher was as steady as a wall of brass. Look for look he repaid the contemptuous smile of Dr. Morgan.

"Pick out another course, if you like," said he. "I've made my suggestion, but please yourself!"

Dr. Morgan shook his head.

"I don't think so," said he. "There's no use. I see that you've beaten me before the race begins. Why, man, you ought to know that nobody in the world can ride that roan devil except Sandy Sweyn, and Sandy weighs a full two hundred and twenty pounds. Aye, or a little bit more! But we'll have the pleasure of seeing how fast Cleo *can* run. Are you ready?"

"I'm ready."

"Just fire your pistol to give them the word. Sandy, it's to be around that black rock —

the one with the three heads on it. Do you see?"

"I see."

"Ride hard — but not too hard, Sandy. You can't beat the gelding. But try not to be disgraced!"

"Beat the gelding?" said Sandy Sweyn. "Why, there ain't no trouble about that. Even if he had four good legs under him, there wouldn't be no trouble about that. I'll catch him at the rock, and I'll walk away from him coming back."

With one ear the rancher overheard the amazing confidence of this remark, but the greater portion of his attention was given to instructing his jockey.

"Get the big boy going and keep him at it. Not too much of the spurs. He hates the spurs except when *I'm* using them, and then I *make* him like 'em. Use the quirt. Put a little spice in the loafer."

"I'll run his head off and make that plow horse sick in a quarter of a mile. The doctor is a nut to put a bet on a race like this," said the gentle Shorty. "Give us the signal to start, will you?"

# 4

The start was in line with the big derrick above the haystack, and the finish was to be at the same line. The spectators scattered themselves in various places of vantage, more particularly upon the top of the stack, on the table of the hay press, and one daring fellow — the roust-about of the baling crew — clambered out and sat on the swing tip of the derrick's boom, to the envy and admiration of all of the rest.

In this manner, they got a view of the course from the moment that the rancher's gun exploded and the two darted off over the sun-burned fields.

The yell that greeted that start was followed by a groan from the hay-press crew. They saw that their favorite was not only under the disadvantage of seventy pounds of extra weight, but also she was forced to run in going that was worse than that of the gelding. That lithe racer with the lighter burden of Shorty in the saddle, went lightly across the hay stubble, but the tremendously pounding hoofs of the roan broke through the crust and raised puffs of dust and clotted soil at every fling of her hoofs.

"We're beat — we're cheated!" said the bale roller with a groan.

"Steady!" answered Dr. Morgan. "Let's not whimper when we pay. They'd rather have us whine than take our money."

The faces of the hay-press men set like iron, while the doctor smiled almost benignantly down upon Peter Dunstan. Who could have guessed from the doctor's face that rage and scorn and regret were tearing his heart?

He managed to say amiably:

"Cleo will beat your horse yet, Dunstan."

"Well!" muttered the tall rancher, "I wouldn't believe that there was that much go in any horse of that cut — with as much weight on her back!"

The doctor looked across the field carelessly. Then his heart leaped fairly into his throat. He had not more than pretended to stare after the two sweeping forms.

Now what he saw was the gelding, stretched out true and straight in the height of his speed, with Shorty raised in the stirrups and bent forward along the neck of his mount, jockeying him along to take the full advantage of every effort that the fine animal made.

In the saddle of Cleo, the stolid form of big Sandy Sweyn sat erect, as though he had no more than the most indifferent interest in this race. Yet the reaching nose of the big mare was upon the hip of the gelding, and she maintained her place fairly as they swept out of view behind the rock.

There was the utter silence of complete wonder from the watchers in the distance. There was the silence of despair in the heart of Shorty as he jerked the gelding short around the rock and headed him for the home goal.

The pounding monster had remained at his hip all the way to the rock, and a horrible dread was in Shorty that the promise of the half-wit to his old master would be performed.

He straightened the gelding toward the haystack three quarters of a mile away. The quirt hissed and bit the flank of the gallant beast; in answer there was only a convulsive jerking of the body of the gelding — sure proof that the whip cut him, but that he could not answer with a greater burst of speed.

At that very moment, as the pride of all the Dunstan horses launched out at fullest speed, the monstrous roan mare drew up beside — a blue roan — like a gleaming blue shadow, with the red of polished granite shining through. The very ground shook under the beat of her hoofs, and she was gaining steadily. Then Sandy Sweyn leaned a little in the saddle, and as he swayed forward, he seemed to make the great mare stumble into redoubled speed.

At every jump the distance between the two riders was jerked to a greater and greater stretch. Shorty, screaming like a soul in torment, yelled:

"You fool! You fool! Are you gunna beat the hoss and the bet of your own boss?"

The big man turned in the saddle, and Shorty had sight of a vague, uncomprehending face. No need to try this villainous temptation in a place where it would not even be understood! Shorty bowed his head with another groan and resigned himself to his fate — to come in eating the dust of this monstrous beast and his half-witted rider!

Still the great blue roan drifted farther and farther away. He knew horses, did Shorty, and with an anxious eye he waited to see her pounding in weariness in her stride — waited to see her head go up. Many and many a time as he stood in the stands, with his bets placed, had Shorty seen the thoroughbreds come storming down the stretch. Many times he had seen the head of the spent horse jerk up and begin to bob like a cork in a wild-running stream. For that sign he waited now — or to see the mare bear out to one side or another.

There was not a hint of such a change. Suddenly Shorty knew definitely that there would *not* be such a change. There was an untapped well of incredible strength in her that had not yet been called upon. Sandy Sweyn sat, only slightly pitched forward in the saddle to break the wind of the galloping and to swing him with the swing of the mare.

Just as that moment of bitterness swelled in the heart of Shorty, he saw the head of the gelding jerk high. At the same instant, there was a wrench and a horrible sinking of the body of the fine horse. Here he was halting and limping, a furlong from the finish line over which the great mare was soon bounding.

The yell of despair from the throats of his fellow punchers was like a dirge to the ear of Shorty; and the shout of joy from the hay balers was a knife thrust of agony.

He slid from the saddle and walked gloomily on, leading the broken horse behind him. He would have been moved to the wildest curses, if there had not been something else that awakened a greater emotion than wrath and shame. That was the sense of superstitious awe.

For the shoulder in which the gelding had gone lame was the one in which the half-wit had declared that he had found a weakness before the race even so much as began. Into that shoulder he had thrust his forefinger, and had seemed to find an over-sensitive spot.

Shorty found this too much for him. He walked in with a face that was a picture of silent and gloomy awe.

Into the uproar he walked. The checks had been handed over to the doctor; the balers had collected the cash of the punchers. On the one side there was a wild rejoicing; on the other side there was a bitter gloom.

The laughter and the cursing died away on both sides, as the limping gelding hobbled in among them. What a picture between the dancing creature that had started in the race and this which hobbled home at the finish of it.

"If I had had a *real* rider —" said big Peter Dunstan savagely.

Shorty turned upon him with murder in his eye.

"If you'd of had the sense of a half-wit," said he, "you would never of started a cripple in a race like this!"

Peter Dunstan was a man of great passion, but there had never been a moment since his childhood when he had allowed a bad temper to decide his action to his own harm. Now he merely looked Shorty steadily in the eye; and then he added:

"You're pretty hot, Shorty, and I'm not going to talk to you now. You run along and try to raise enough wind to cool yourself."

"Take that horse out and sink a chunk of lead through its brain, Harry," said he to one of the punchers. "It'll never be any good to any other man. And it's cost me enough money by going lame *once*. I won't have it turn that trick on me again!"

Harry took the reins — then paused to strip the saddle off the back of the tall horse, which stood with head hanging in weariness and in pain.

"Look here," said a voice from the distance, a drawling, slowly monotonous voice, "there *is* something that could be done for that shoulder."

They turned to find big Sandy Sweyn approaching — with the shadowy blue roan at his heels.

"Are you a doctor, son?" asked the big rancher sternly.

"Dunstan," broke in Dr. Morgan, "remember that if he has cost you five thousand today, he may be the saving of ten times that much to you later on. Don't throw him away!"

"Now I'm going to turn this horse over to you, kid," Dunstan said after mastering his anger. "If you know where the lameness is in that leg, I'll leave it to you to cure him of the limp, and do a good job of it, too!"

For a fortnight Dunstan did not leave the new place. There was much to be done there

— very much indeed, if he wished to have good pasture for his cows that winter. Every day he was in the saddle from morning until the night. Every night he sat up until after the middle hour, writing letters in a swift, bold, illegible hand, while the moths fluttered in white showers around his lamp and cast upon his letter paper the oily dust from their wings.

There was nothing but bitter hard labor in all the changes which he had to initiate, but there was an infinite satisfaction to the rancher. He had one touch of amusement, too, three days after he arrived.

He was out with two of his men to supervise the construction of an artificial "tank" which might serve as a watering place for his cows. As they came over a hill, they heard the thunderous bellowing of two fighting bulls. Then they saw them in the hollow — one, the great, red Durham of the doctor's breeding, already with flanks withering from famine, the other a hardy range bull, with a front, scarred by many a hard conflict of a similar nature.

He could not, for a moment, endure the plunging weight of the red bull, however. Back he went, staggering, his knees sagging.

"He's going down and out!" said one of the punchers.

"Bah," said the rancher, "he's hardly

started to fight. Wait till he gets warmed up, and he'll make that hand-fed fatty grunt, I can tell you!"

He was right. The range bull disengaged his horns, leaped to the side, and the red monster went floundering past. Before he could change the direction of his charge the agile hero of the mountain desert had caught him full in the tender flank with ripping, goring horns.

One touch of that pepper was enough for the Durham. He fled for his life, bellowing twice as loud with pain and fear as he had ever done with rage before. After him went the range bull, far fleeter of foot, and plowing up the crimson flanks of the Durham with repeated thrusts.

Peter Dunstan enjoyed the sight with a grim smile.

"Shall I drive 'em apart?" asked one of the men, as the pair disappeared over the next swell of the land.

"Let 'em go!" replied the rancher. "If you save that fat fool of a prize bull to-day, he'll be butchered to-morrow. I wouldn't have such stock on my range, I tell you!"

He went on, content. He only wished, in his heart of hearts, that he could have had the doctor at hand to see that combat and its result.

When the fortnight ended, and the rancher decided that it was time for him to hurry back to the home place, he came upon a most unpleasant spectacle.

It was old Buck, the same range bull who had conquered the Durham on that other day — now lying on his side upon the plain, dead. He was terribly cut up, and the spot, where the horn of the victorious bull had plunged through his side and found the heart, was plainly visible.

"But what bull could have done it?" asked Peter Dunstan. "Unless one of the youngsters got in a lucky crack at Buck, I can't explain it, because none of the old fellows are foolish enough to even lock horns with him. He's given a lesson to all of them."

Indeed, he was the lord and the patriarch of the Dunstan herds, and he had carved the fear of himself with dreadful horns on all the thousands of cattle that roamed upon that section of the range.

The explanation was not far to seek. They had not ridden on a mile and a half before they came upon a mighty bull, sunk to the belly in the cool wallowing mud at the verge of a "tank." The red of battle was not yet washed away from his front. His horns were painted from the war, and his sides were covered and crisscrossed by the black markings of wounds, recently received.

When he saw the riders, he backed from the mud and whirled upon them with the angry roar of a truly vicious bull. Lofty at the withers as a buffalo, ponderous of shoulder and of haunch also, his eyes two balls of red fire, his flanks wrinkled, and his belly tucked up from the scant fare on which he had been living, who could have told that this was the great Durham bull of the doctor's breeding?

He charged them with a bellow of madness, and Peter Dunstan put spurs to his horse and rode away without a word. He did not like to have his predictions turn out so far from correct. Not one of the punchers behind him dared to voice a comment. But when they came back to the ranch house they had quite an interesting story to tell!

However, Peter Dunstan was in a quandary. He had announced before all his best men that the red Durham bull was a worthless thing and that he did not want it on his range. Now he had changed his mind, but could he afford to cast aside dignity and infallibility, with his punchers realizing it?

He would not have done so had it not been for the loss of the famous Buck. That was a grand bull, a perfect type for the range, according to Peter Dunstan. He could not very well accept that loss without taking some steps to replace it.

Here was the red bull, growing thinner and thinner with the passage of every day. He had proved the might of his limbs, the courage of his heart, and the readiness with which he could learn the lessons of battle. Still, he was starving to death! He had lived too long in reach of all the hay he could eat and cool water to drink. He could not forage for himself.

The thought of that great red bull haunted Mr. Dunstan all the way back to the old ranch house.

He got there in the middle of afternoon and found, sitting on the corral fence, whittling, the bulky shoulders and the thoughtless face of Sandy Sweyn, his hat pushed far back on his head.

"Well!" cried the boss. "Is *that* all that you can find to do? Hasn't Steve sent you to do something?"

The half-wit raised his dull, handsome face, and shook his head.

It had been the rancher's idea of an easy job for the simple fellow to make him roust-about to his formidable cook. Steve McGuire's mulligan stew was famous across the width and up and down the length of the range. The length of his punching arm and the hardness of his fist was famous, also. It was never possible to keep an assistant with Steve for more than a very short period indeed. Surely it was more than wonderful if Steve were not able to keep the half-wit busy from the dawn to the dark.

"No," said Sandy Sweyn, "he didn't seem to need me none."

"He didn't seem?" cried the rancher. "Did you *ask* him?"

"Sure," said Sandy Sweyn, with large and innocent eyes. "I asked him, and he said that he didn't need me."

"Did he tell you to come out here and sit on the fence like a scarecrow?"

Sandy Sweyn concentrated his far-away eyes in recollection.

"He said that he didn't give a hang what I did," said Sandy and then nodded, pleased with the flawless accuracy of his memory. "Yes, that's what he said."

"I'm going to ask Steve," said the rancher, "and if you're lying, you'll regret it!"

He got to the kitchen door in two bounds of his spur-tortured horse. He flung himself from the saddle and quickly strode through the kitchen door.

"Hey!" yelled a giant voice. "What d'you mean by letting the dust in on this here coffee cake, you long-legged shorthorn? Who asked you to step into this here kitchen, Dunstan?"

Peter Dunstan, abashed, closed the door hastily behind him, and watched the last of the dust which he had admitted settling on the surface of the twisted rolls of coffee cake. There was never a breakfast without those cakes. It sweetened all the life on the ranch for Dunstan and his men.

He said mildly: "I only came to ask you, Steve, if you knew that your roustabout was sitting on the corral fence?"

# 5

With a glare Steve McGuire paused in his slicing of the coffee cake, preparatory to strewing the sliced walnuts over its sticky surface.

"Is he setting on the fence?" quoth Steve. "All I wish is that he was setting on the edge of a cliff, instead, and that there was a wind strong enough to blow him over the edge. All I wish is that there was a thousand-foot drop on the off side of that cliff, and that the rocks was hard below and just enough river to wash away the dust from the spot where he landed. Outside of that, there ain't much harm that I wish to him."

"He wouldn't work?" asked Mr. Dunstan. "Then there are ways of *making* him work!"

"Wouldn't?" echoed the cook. "Oh, he would work, well enough. He was plumb willing. But he *couldn't* work. Look yonder, I ask you, at what's left of the best cleaver that a butcher ever swung! How many steers and how many deer have I broke up with that cleaver? And now look at it!"

He took down from the wall a monstrous cleaver, larger and heavier than a woodsman's ax. Behold, all the biting edge had been stripped from the face of the tool!

"How the devil did *that* happen?" asked the rancher.

"*I* dunno," answered the cook sadly, turning the cleaver gloomily from side to side. "Look at the balance that it's got? And look at the make of it! That was the best German steel that was ever made. Why, you could stand all day long and bust up *rocks* with that cleaver. And it wouldn't even have its edge turned. I gave it to Sandy Sweyn to cut up a quarter of beef. He give two whacks. Then I hear a sort of a terrible pounding begin that made the house fair shake. I yells out:

" 'What are you doing?'

"He says: 'This here cleaver seems to be sort of broke.'

"I didn't believe that it was possible. I went in and I seen that he had smashed the edges of that cleaver like it was made of glass, not of steel at all! How he done it, I dunno. But he ain't human. He's got the strength of ten mules locked up in that right arm of his and ten wild hosses is in his *left* hand. And you never know when you ask for something if them twenty animals ain't gunna come a-ragin' out and trample right on over you."

The rancher took the cleaver, examined it, and passed it back, filled with wonder rather than with anger. He himself had swung that cleaver. He knew the strength of that steel. How dreadful, then, must have been the might of the man who had driven the cleaver with such force that it had shattered the entire edge upon the ox bone.

"You could let him do something that takes no sense, Steve," he suggested. "You could let him chop the wood for your fire, for you. You're always saying that it takes half of your time for the chopping of the wood, you know!"

Steve McGuire strode to the wall. He took down from it three axes. The handle of one was splintered to matchwood. Another was broken across and across. The handle of the third was wrapped round and round with linen tape. Even so, the fracture was visible through the bandaging.

"All the finest kind of steel. You know the kind of axes that I've always made you buy for me, Dunstan. Them handles was the finest hickory that ever was growed. I ain't no baby when it comes to the swinging of an ax. Not me! I've had the picking of those handles myself, and I know wood. But this fool — this blockhead, that you sent to me, he took them three axes of mine, and he went out to cut me up some wood.

"He cut me up two big armfuls mighty

quick. I looked out through the window after he brought in the first armful, and I seen him working on that wood. It was all oak. All twisted and seasoned scrub oak, just one mite harder and meaner than iron is, to work up, but the way that feller was swingin' that ax, he was just sinking it through that oak as though it was dough.

"I yelled out: 'Hey, don't bust that ax!' because it scared me to see the way that he was sinking that ax as though it was soft white pine that he was handling. Well, sir, that yell of mine sort of startled him, and he gave that stroke extra hard. Smash went the handle. There it is now — the one that looks as though a lion had spent the afternoon chewing it up for fun! No, Mr. Dunstan, I am not a very particular sort of a man, but I could put up with busted tools where I couldn't put up with bein' burned alive, and that's what pretty near happened!"

Peter Dunstan sat down in amazement and asked for fuller particulars and now some great black, burned patches on the floor were shown to him.

"I tell that fool to put some fresh wood in the fire. He does. But he gets a hold of a chunk of wood that he had cut with whiskers on it, and the whiskers make it so big that it won't fit into the stove.

"He turns around to me with the smoke pourin' out into the kitchen and spoilin' everything and he says: 'Steve, this here stick it don't seem to fit very well.'

" 'You dunderhead!' I yells at him. 'Ain't you able to jam it in?'

" 'I'll do my best,' says he in that fool, mild way of his, and he does!

"That was what he done, too. He *jammed* it in. He give it a shove and there wasn't quite room. And then he braced one hand agin' the wall and he give the stick *another* shove, and this time, I can tell you that something moved. That stove buckled like a shell had exploded on the inside of it, and it comes down smash and leaves a lot of red-hot coals go rolling across on the floor.

"It was a terrible job. I got so choked with smoke that I couldn't do a thing, and had to go and hang my head out of the window to get some fresh air. While I was doing that, the house pretty near burned down. And it *would* of burned down, except that that fool, he don't care what sort of air he has to breathe. He just out and clears up them burning sticks and tramples the sparks out, and then he helps me to set up the stove again — him doing wrong everything that I start to do right.

"Pretty soon I give him a yell and grabbed up a frying pan and slammed him with it. I thought that it would of brained him, but it was pretty near wore out, and it busted all to pieces. He just stood there rubbing his head and looking at me sort of mild and surprised that way that he has. Then I told him to get out, and he got."

The rancher listened to this long narrative with wonder.

Then he walked in thought back to the corral. He had his promise to the doctor in his mind, but to maintain in the ranch a youth who was incapable of service was a thought that goaded the rancher to the very heart. Waste — purest waste — and it was not upon such principles as these that his success in life had been based.

He stood, at last, before the stolid figure on the fence.

"What about the horse, Sandy?" he asked. "I suppose that the gelding is in his grave by this time. I suppose that after you got through taking care of him, he was about ready to feed the buzzards?"

"No," said Sandy, "he ain't meant for the buzzards. Would you like to see him?"

"See him? Yes, where do you keep him?"

"Right here."

He whistled, a sharp, thin note that was answered by the beat of hoofs at once. From behind the shed, a horse came at a gallop.

It was the gelding, with all the limp gone from his gallop, and the lame shoulder doing its full share of service without a perceptible flaw.

"Look out!" cried Mr. Dunstan, in even more alarm than wonder, as he saw the savage horse come straight up behind the half-wit. "Look out, Sandy, or he'll tear your head off —"

"Why should he?" asked Sandy blandly. "Him and me are pretty good friends. Ain't we, old timer?"

He stretched out his arm, and the long head and neck of the gelding were passed that moment beneath it. There he stood, with pricking ears and a happy light in his eyes which the rancher had never seen there before.

"Confound it!" said Peter Dunstan, "how did you manage to tame that brute?"

"I'll tell you," said Sandy Sweyn thoughtfully. "All he needed was somebody to talk to that he could understand. You see?"

"Talk to? You mean to say that he could understand you — and you could understand him?"

"Oh, yes."

"What lingo did he speak?"

"Not words," explained Sandy Sweyn. "But there is a different sort of a language for everything, you know. Only, you got to sort of open up your mind" — he made a wide gesture — "then, you sort of get in touch — you understand?"

The thin scream of a hawk floated down from above and slid coldly into the soul of Peter Dunstan in the pause that followed. He wanted to laugh but dared not.

"Do you understand *that?*" he asked, and pointed up.

"Sure," said Sandy Sweyn. "And he'll understand me."

He placed both his thumbs in his mouth and then emitted a piercing, half-vocal whistle that tore through the air and drove up — until it seemed to strike the floating hawk like a bullet. In one swoop the preying bird sagged half the distance toward the earth and then hung on what Peter Dunstan would have liked to call — a listening wing.

One might say that Mr. Peter Dunstan found himself in a stupid position. He stood with mouth wide open, his face bearing a stricken look. When he glanced at Sandy Sweyn again, he saw that that young man had seemingly forgotten all about the hawk that he had whistled out of the sky. He was now rubbing the nose of the gelding with an affectionate hand.

For the first time in Peter Dunstan's life, there arose before his mind a strange premonition of events and things beyond all common seeing and all common hearing.

Mr. Dunstan shut the door of his mind upon these uncanny emotions and mental hints.

"Saddle that gelding for me, Sandy," said he. "Saddle that gelding for me, because I'm going to try him out right now. It's not *possible* that he's cured so completely and so soon. Saddle him, and bring him to the door of the house. Then whistle to let me know that you're there."

With this, Peter Dunstan returned to the house. There he found Steve McGuire with a pan between his knees, into which he dropped potato after potato, as fast as his hands could slice away their brown covers and turn them to a crystal-shining white.

"Now, Steve," said the rancher, "I want you to tell me what that half-wit has been doing to cure the lame shoulder of the gelding?"

"What has he been doing?" echoed Steve McGuire, with a frown. "All I know is that he went out, got an armful of weeds and stuff from the hills, came back, stewed them up in a wash boiler, and filled the house with an odor that hasn't washed out or aired out yet! And he's taken that stuff and used it to rub into the shoulder of the horse. It ought to of killed the poor brute or cured it. And if it's cured, it's because the nerves in its nose ain't sensitive none!"

Mr. Peter Dunstan sighed with relief.

"There's no miracle about it, then," said he. "Just a simple matter of herbs."

Steve sniffed loudly, then asked, "But where did he learn to doctor up animals like that?"

"From Dr. Morgan, of course," said Dunstan.

But he did not believe what he said.

"He gentled that crazy brute of a horse that I've been fighting every time I get on his back," said Dunstan.

"Would you call him a gentle hoss now?" asked Steve, putting his head to one side. "If you had seen him make a dive at me when I was coming back from the barn with a hatful of eggs the other day, you wouldn't be saying that he was gentled none. No, sir. He made a pass at me with his teeth just as I was diving through the bars of the fence and he pretty near tore the seat out of my trousers. I squashed a dozen eggs all over myself!"

"Bah!" said Peter Dunstan. "He has the horse so gentle that it comes running to his whistle. More like a confounded dog than anything else. I'm going to ride the horse now and see how he is."

"You are going to ride him now?" said Steve McGuire. "Well, Dunstan, I'm telling you right here and now that that Sandy Sweyn ain't the kind that will ever do many useful things for other folks. The tricks that he turns might have some sort of use for himself, but not for no others. I'll bet you that you'll find that hoss has got something wrong with him."

"Man," said the rancher, "haven't I seen him with my own eyes, galloping as fast as he ever did in his life? A smoother action than he had the day that the roan mare with a ton of fool on her back was able to run away from him. I'll ride the gelding. You come and watch."

"Captain," said Steve McGuire, "that's just the thing that I'm gunna do!"

There was a wicked light in the eye of Steve as he stepped to the door and peered at the gelding Sandy led up to the house. While Sandy stood at the head of the horse, Mr. Dunstan mounted with more ease than he had ever found possible on all of the occasions when he swung himself upon the back of the same animal in the past.

He had time to settle his feet in the stirrups and freshen the grip of his knees. If the ears of the gelding flickered back for an instant, they pricked forward again at once, for the hand of Sandy Sweyn was gently rubbing his velvety nose.

Said Sandy: "He ain't feeling right, Mr. Dunstan."

"Who told you that?" asked Dunstan.

"He ain't feeling right in his mind."

"About what?"

"About you," said Sandy.

"I'll mend that," said Peter Dunstan. "Stand away from his head, will you?"

No sooner said than done. Sandy Sweyn stepped back to one side, and the gelding stepped the other way, and stepped into the air at the same time.

He gave himself a twist around while he was off terra firma, such a violent twist that one of Mr. Dunstan's feet was disengaged from the stirrup. Before that foot could find its place again, the horse landed with all his force upon one stiffened foreleg. It happened that the side on which the leg came down was that on which Mr. Dunstan had already lost the stirrup.

He was a fine rider and in ordinary circumstances he would have kept his seat in spite of such bucking. But the lost stirrup was against him. The force of gravity and the gelding worked in beautiful accord, and Peter Dunstan crashed to the ground.

His courage was not daunted. While he was flying through mid-air he was already yelling: "Stop him! Head him! Don't let him get away —"

He rose with his face badly scratched, his

shoulder almost dislocated, and a handful of sand sifting up and down between his shirt and his skin. Then he saw that there was no need to ride in pursuit of the gelding. It stood with Sandy Sweyn as a sort of bulwark between it and the rancher, eying him with a bright, big-eyed curiosity over the shoulder of the half-wit.

Mr. Dunstan flung down his hat and kicked it farther away from him.

"I'll ride that horse or break his neck — or let him break mine!" he shouted in a white heat.

For he had conquered that horse before, and it is intolerable to even dream that what we have once beaten cannot be controlled again.

Once more the rancher rushed and found himself in the saddle. He took a firm toe hold on the stirrups. A glittering devil shone from his eyes. "Let him go!" he shouted to Sandy Sweyn.

As Sandy Sweyn removed his hand from the bridle of the gelding, the same phenomenon was repeated. The mild, bright eyes of the gelding grew as wicked as those of his rider. His head turned into a snaky, ominous thing. He left the earth as though he intended to live in air for a while.

He did not fight in a foolish passion but with a wicked malice.

Mr. Dunstan was a fine rider, as has been said before, but he was mortal. Finally he swung far out to the side.

At that very moment the gelding chose to buck jump in the opposite direction, checking his swing with a wonderful skill. It was as though the saddle had been snatched from beneath Mr. Dunstan. He was not slung from the saddle. He even seemed to hang for an instant in midair. He fell only a scant six feet, but that fall was solid and compact, so to speak.

He fell upon his side, rolled upon his back limply and lay still with each fist clenched, but with his wide eyes blank.

Sandy Sweyn stood entranced in wonder. The yell of the cook did not rouse him. As the gelding ran to him again, he began to smooth the shining neck of the horse and murmur little, soothing, wordless words.

Steve McGuire, in the meantime, was busy fetching water. He drenched Peter Dunstan from head to foot. Still the rancher did not stir. He strove to lift his boss in his strong arms. But two hundred limp pounds are an almost impossible burden even for a strong man to manage, unless he knows the knack of it. Steve McGuire was more a master in the art of flooring men than in that of lifting them up again.

Strength of wits seemed to come to Sandy Sweyn at last.

He advanced and brushed the cook lightly to one side. As Steve explained afterward to a friend, it was as though a twisted bar of living steel — if such a thing can be imagined — had touched against him, with a mighty engine propelling it.

Sandy Sweyn stooped and picked up the fallen man lightly. He advanced to the kitchen door; he shifted his burden, and supporting it in one arm, as a father might support a slender child, with his free hand he opened the door and so passed on into the house.

Steve recovered his senses at last and showed the way to a bed. There the master of the ranch was laid.

A minute later he opened his eyes — closed them — and when they were opened again, they were lighted with full understanding of all that had passed. They rested upon Sandy Sweyn's blank face for a long moment.

"There's a bull running amuck on my range, Sandy," said he. "A big, red Durham bull that used to belong to your friend, the doctor. Go out and bring it in. There's a ring already in its nose!"

# 6

Making no comment, Sandy Sweyn turned in perfect good humor and left the house.

"How are you, chief?" said Steve.

"Beaten," said the rancher, "plain beaten, Steve."

Steve McGuire flushed.

"If I had knowed that the hoss was as plumb bad as all that —"

That was the nearest that he could come to an apology. But Dunstan broke in: "Oh, I don't mean the horse."

Before Steve could answer with a question, his eye fell upon a form beyond the window and he exclaimed:

"Blast me, Dunstan, if the fool ain't starting out *on foot!*"

The reply of the rancher turned him to stone.

"I knew he would!" said Dunstan.

"Knew that he would?" cried Steve McGuire. "Why, man, man, that there red bull has been tearing up the range. He killed the big —"

"I know. I saw the body."

"He'll murder the boy, chief!"

"There'll be one fool less in the world," said Dunstan coldly. "No, what I'm after is to find out if this Sandy Sweyn is really just a man that has a sort of power over animals — or if he's really queer!"

"Queer?" echoed Steve.

"I mean that." He raised himself from the bed and sat down in a chair by the window. Apparently his mind was so intent on the problem that occupied it that he had quite forgotten his badly bruised body.

"I used to hold that horse in the hollow of my hand, Steve."

"He was always a good deal of a handful," said Steve. "But I've seen you make him like it."

"But to-day he was changed. He was like a crazy thing, Steve. Not crazy, either. He seemed to be fighting with brains. If a man's brain had the body of a horse to use, he might have fought something like that!"

A little chill struck through the honest brain of Steve McGuire.

"Chief, what're you're driving at?"

Mr. Dunstan rolled a cigarette.

"I hardly just know," said he. "But look here. We know that this Sweyn has done queer things with the roan and with the gelding. That may mean that he has only a trick with

73

horses. And a good many people have been able to do something like that. But what is the biggest fool thing in the world? A bull, Steve.

"There's no sense to it at all, when it gets its temper up. That Durham has its temper up. Its sides are gashed, and the wounds not healed. It's made a kill, and it's the king of the range. Now, Steve, I tell you that if this half-wit can bring in the red bull, there *is* something queer about him; so queer that I'll believe that he was able to put something into the mind of the gelding and show him how to pitch me on my head! We'll wait, and we'll see."

The late afternoon sank into the amber evening; the amber turned to red gold; the red gold died to rose and crimson and orange and streaks of green. All of this turned to softly colored dusk, and dusk waned to twilight; then across the pure face of the night the last small stars drew down in droves and in clusters. Still there was no sign of Sandy Sweyn.

Shorty rose in the bunk house and looked through the open window. He said: "I am gunna wait until mornin'. And if the kid ain't come in by that time, I'm gunna ride to town. And if the sheriff wants a posse to bring in the boss of this here ranch, I'm gunna be the first volunteer."

He turned upon his heel and stood in the doorway with his thumbs hooked in his belt. He said to the open and solemn face of the night:

"Not that I give a hang about that fool-faced kid. But there's really such a thing in this wide world as a truly square deal —"

He left that thought unfinished. Because, in truth, it did not need any great amount of finishing. The rest made not a comment. The lantern was put out, some half hour later, and the first snore was making its trembling beginning, when another deep voice spoke out of the dark in a rumble:

"And me, I'm gunna ride right in at your side, Shorty, old-timer. There ain't nobody has got a right to act like a king. Not in this here country. Not in this here century!"

Let no one think that Peter Dunstan did not realize very well just what was passing in the minds of his men. In the middle of the night, his sleepless mind tormented him to such a point that he rose, in spite of his aching nerves, and went out to the corral where his own saddle string was kept by itself, because he would not have his high-blooded horses mixed with others. A thousand-dollar blooded horse can be spoiled by a kick as easily as any fifty-dollar mustang.

He chose an easy-gaited brown mare. Since

there was no one to see and comment, he could make this concession to his aching bones and to his bruised muscles. He saddled that horse and rode forth through the night, straight toward the spot at which he had seen the red bull the same day. Because, to his thinking, it was unlikely that the bull, untrained in the ways of the range, would wander far from the same spot, where the water of the near-by tank would tempt him to remain.

He rode freely, and he rode fast, but the distance was long. On the way, the moon stepped above the eastern horizon line and looked him in the face.

That slanting light turned the quiet face of the broad tank into a sheet of solid silver, when at last he came into sight of it. The next thing that he made out was the great black silhouette of the bull against that bright background.

He rode a little closer. There was something white on the dark of the ground, and a shadowy outline beneath the moon — the form of a man!

The heart of Peter Dunstan seemed to stop in his breast. He reined his horse to a standstill. There lay the motionless form of a man, not ten feet from the grazing bull. The dead body of Sandy Sweyn, of course! Across the brain of the rancher swarmed sudden and frightful pictures. For the first time, keenly, he was aware of how much the honest respect of his neighbors and his men meant to him. Beside their respect and beyond it, there was the dreadful arm of the law. What would the law say to a case of this sort — where a poor half-witted youngster, a poor mental child was the victim?

At least, he would put a period to the bull's existence! At that instant it saw him, too. Up flashed its tail and down sank its head. It rushed thirty steps nearer, and paused to snort at the earth and send low, long billows of dust rolling away on either side. It stamped and pawed the earth with mighty strokes. In the meantime, giving the rancher all the time that he needed to draw his bead and make sure of his target with a perfect bead!

His trigger finger was already curling softly about the trigger. Death was not a tenth of a second away from the Durham bull, when a mild voice said, not far away:

"Hello, who's there?"

The voice of Sandy Sweyn!

Behold, he has advanced to the side of the bull. He stands with one hand resting lightly upon the horns where the blood of the day's victim is still black and stiff.

"Hello, Mr. Dunstan. It's a grand, bright night, ain't it? I stayed out here to sort of enjoy it. There ain't no breathing in a house, you know!"

In the gray of the morning, when the punchers turned out from their bunks, they were aware of the big outline of their boss riding in toward the house. Shorty, himself, hailed Peter Dunstan.

"Has the half-wit turned up yet, Mr. Dunstan?"

"The devil with the half-wit!" bellowed Peter Dunstan. And he hastily rode on.

That was why five Colts were piled and looked to with care in the bunkhouse before the men went in to their breakfast. As they sat about the table, there was a hoarse roar from Steve McGuire. What he said was not instantly made out, but it caused a rush to the windows. There they saw one of the strangest spectacles that ever the eye of a good Westerner rested upon.

They saw the giant Durham bull meandering slowly in, pausing to crop a bunch of grass of favorable appearance, from time to time; some fifty yards ahead of him, strolling along with an equal unconcern, walked none other than young Sandy Sweyn!

No man spoke. It was a thing to be expressed only in muted curses. Who could find the right words to apply to such a picture?

To have said that the bull was following

the man at heel like a dog would have been an absurdity, a thing never to be believed. Yet what else was happening, if this were not the fact? The great red bull at the rear of the youth passed toward one of the corrals and entered it with a strange meekness. They saw the bars put up. They saw a quantity of hay taken from the shed and pitched down in a corner for the hungry beast to feed upon. They saw Sandy Sweyn then place his hand upon the top bar of the fence and vault over it with as much ease as though a great beat of wings were floating him across it.

What seemed, to some of them, strangest of all was that the hollow-sided bull, in spite of his famine, straight-way left the hay and ran to the corral fence, pawing the ground into clouds of dust as he bellowed forth a thunderous call after Sandy. Sandy turned near the house and spoke a few words which had no sense at all, but which changed the restlessness of the big bull into perfect passivity.

The bull went back toward his hay, and Sandy entered the kitchen.

"He's promised to come back and see that brute again," said somebody.

The others glared askance at the speaker, for the same absurd idea had entered every brain, and a cowpuncher is not used to attributing brains to beef.

They heard Sandy in the kitchen asking the cook if he were too late for breakfast, and they heard big Steve McGuire grumblingly admit that he had something for the boy to eat.

Quality was not essential to big Sandy Sweyn, but quantity was a prime requisite. Peter Dunstan, who hated waste, was nevertheless not unwilling to feed a man who had turned a terrible menace on his range into a valuable piece of property quietly in hand in the corral near the house.

The other punchers wandered out toward the day's work, but Peter Dunstan made pause in the kitchen.

"What's that beef that I saw in the meat house, Steve?"

"A yearling that Buck got."

"That infernal bear! How did it happen?"

"I don't know. The same that usually happens. The boys was close enough to hear the bawl of the calf chopped off short in the middle by a blow that sounded like a whang on a bass drum. When they come up, Buck wasn't waiting for them, but there were his tracks leading away through the brush. And there was the calf, dead on the ground, with his ribs along one side smashed in flat."

"They didn't follow the trail?"

"What's the good?" said Steve. "They've

follered his trail a hundred times and never got nothing out of it. Ain't you follered it ten times yourself, Dunstan?"

It is very bad for a man when he has no vent for healthy rage. Mr. Dunstan, striding back into the dining room, glared down at Sandy Sweyn.

He saw the eyes of the youth widen, and his color altered a little. He half choked upon a great chunk of bread.

"Sandy," said Peter Dunstan, "I have a job for you."

Gloom descended upon the features of Sandy Sweyn.

"What would be a job for anybody else," said the rancher, "but I think that you would like it. It's to go off by yourself for as long as you like, and bring me back a grizzly's hide."

The gloom lifted from the face of Sandy Sweyn.

"Oh," said Sandy, "I'll start after breakfast and a nap."

"You'll find my rifles in the front room," said Peter Dunstan. "And you can take the one that you like the best. Take your pick of saddles, too. And the roan will —"

"Why," said Sandy Sweyn, "hosses throw a scent farther than a man does. And a rifle is too heavy to carry."

Mr. Dunstan swallowed with some difficulty.

"Are you going to spend the season *trapping* him, Sandy?" said he.

"No," said Sandy. "This will shoot hard enough if you get close and hit the right spot."

And he brought out an old-fashioned Colt and laid it on the table, where he regarded it for a long time with the most affectionate eyes.

"Come, come!" said Peter Dunstan. "You'd have to get right on top of him to kill a grizzly with a gun like that — or else you'd have to put a bullet through his eye!"

"Well?" asked Sandy Sweyn.

Peter Dunstan said no more, but he took notice that, according to his speech, Sandy Sweyn took with him neither horse nor rifle when he left the house. Neither would he carry flour or bacon or any of the other necessities of camping.

"Why not?" roared Steve McGuire at him.

"It's a lot of weight," said Sandy in apology. "And if I got a pinch of salt along —"

"You get along," said Steve. "You're too queer to be right!"

Steve said afterward to the boss of the ranch: "There ain't gunna no good come out of him.

If he does you good by killing that bear, like I think that he's gunna do, he'll do you a bigger harm in some other way."

# 7

The direction in which Sandy Sweyn started off was that leading toward the spot where the yearling had been killed by the great grizzly. When he had reached the spot of the killing, he made no attempt to follow up the trail of bruin. Instead, he busied himself for some time with strangely minute details. He regarded the trail, not to follow it, but to make out all of its peculiarities — the length of the two hind paws and the length of the front one — the twisted claw on the right hind foot, and the broken claw on the right front foot; the average length of stride as bruin walked, as he ambled, and as he galloped at full speed.

After this, Sandy Sweyn lay down in a spot where the trees wove a motley pattern of shadow above him, and he thought drowsily upon the problem which lay before him until kind sleep closed his eyes.

He slept until far into the afternoon; when he wakened he was ready to work. Appetite did not bother him. Although Sandy made vast assaults upon the larder when the spirit moved him, he also cared not to eat more than once a day.

But what would be the dictates of the stomach of the great bear — Buck? Roots, cattle killing, sheep raiding, the demolition of an ant hill — indeed, almost anything might be to the point with Buck. What Sandy finally decided upon was the rich stores of berries which could be found loading the bushes of the uplands.

In this direction he turned and made off, not in haste, but with a long, stretching step that never varied. It carried him over, up and down, rough and level, with an equal speed. There were five hours until sundown, and in the five hours he put behind him twenty-five miles — which, over that rough going, would have been a heavy whole day's march for any other man.

He slept again until midnight. Then he was up and marching until dawn.

Here he made his second halt. He had climbed out of the rolling brown hills. He had passed the foothills of the range. Now he was in a chilly region of pines, with great mountain heads going up about him and thronging in the sky, their shoulders partly veiled in the thin lawn of lodge-pole pine, their black throats gleaming in the morning light, their heads now bald, now covered with magnificent white.

Here Sandy Sweyn made a halt again. He knocked over a mountain grouse with a stone. No need to waste a bullet on the stupid, fearless bird. He had that and his cousin roasted for breakfast. Then he climbed into the biggest tree that he could find and surveyed the mountains more clearly, and especially the bottom of the valley.

Then he climbed down and began to make a circuit of the valley. He had not gone four miles before he came on a trail. He could recognize it without stooping to make measurements. It was Buck who, exactly according to the predictions of Sandy, had returned, tired of his cattle raiding, to this more peaceful and congenial work of berrying.

Sandy took two steps, leaped, and caught a branch. Then he pitched himself up among the branches — looking like a madman, so rapidly did he work. Foot and hand were accomplishing only the objects which had been planned by the mind of Sandy, and so he went almost noiselessly up through the tree until, once more, he lay, precariously balanced, and studied the forest beneath him.

There were signs and signs to Sandy Sweyn. The mist which hung upon his mind when other men were near him now lifted a little, and then a little more. He was like one awakening. His glance roved upward, where the eagle tipped and slid sidewise upon great, patient wings as it hung there at watch. He looked downward, where a red squirrel was already venturing down the trunk of the very tree up which he had climbed, going about its business again with the invincible impertinence of its race. Yonder, he saw a bluejay, dipping up and down among the heads of the trees, like a sea bird skimming the waves, scolding at a great rate.

It was so far away that it was only a flashing blue jewel in the morning sun; so far away that ears less marvelous than the ears of Sandy Sweyn would have heard no sign of a sound. He heard, and he guessed at once, what was up.

He climbed down the tree in a manner even stranger than his manner of ascent. As an eagle closes its wings and drops stiff and straight through the air, so Sandy Sweyn stiffened his body and dropped down through the tree, only breaking the speed of his fall by an occasional grip on a branch as he passed. Even the monstrous strength of his arms was tried by those strains.

However, he was on the ground almost as suddenly as though he had descended at a single bound to it. Then he set forward across the forest, abandoning his ordinary walk and breaking into a run. What a speed was that of Sandy Sweyn when he chose to run! Long striding like that of a running horse, smoothly and swiftly, he whipped along with a soundless step, or with only a rustle and a whisper among the grasses to betoken his passing.

He came to the place above which he had seen the bluejay flashing. Though he reached the spot, the bluejay was no longer there. It was a place where a great fallen trunk had been rolled over by the herculean strength of the grizzly, which had then fed upon the worms and the insects that wriggled out at the touch of the strange day. For the stomach of the grizzly is truly omnivorous; nearly all that lives is welcome to his great paunch, particularly when he is lining his ribs with a blanket of fat against the long winter siesta.

After that, he could have followed the trail of the grizzly readily enough across the forest. It is not such a simple matter to follow my lord, the grizzly. Of all the brains that live in the wild, his is the most cunning, just as his paw and his jaw are among the most dreadful in strength. His scent is a keen one, but his power of hearing is a real miracle — almost like the ear of the owl.

Sandy Sweyn did not choose to blunder along such a trail, and perhaps become, presently, the hunted instead of the hunter. For one can never tell what vagary will strike the brain of the grizzly. As he treks steadily along toward the berry beds, his mind may be crossed by the ravishing vision of a certain root patch in the hollow of the valley, or as he heads for the root patch, he may pause to follow a trail of busy ants.

Up another tree went Sandy, but he was hardly at its top when he saw what he wanted. It was not a hundred yards away that the air was turned into confusion. There was a whirlpool of disturbance, a visible movement of the thin air itself, rather than anything palpable. There were tiny specks in movement, and Sandy knew by old experience that this was the swarming of a hive of bees.

The bear was on the trail of honey!

Once more Sandy dropped to the ground through the branches and started for the place ahead of him. He went with more care, since the distance was so short. This time he traveled in a semicircle, so that he would come at the bees against the strong wind which was blowing, and so keep scent and sound of him, if possible, from the bear. As for eyes, the bear is not gifted extraordinarily with them. For that matter, there are no hawk eyes among four-footed creatures, no eyes, even, to match the dull eyes of man, himself.

Sandy made his detour and slid through the

pines until he had an unbroken view of a clearing, just before him, and in the clearing, the outline of a monstrous grizzly reared against the trunk of a tree, and busily tearing it open with his steel talons.

Sandy Sweyn stopped short in the midst of his next step, for he found that he was not the only watcher of the scene. Just before him there was a great, shadowy figure, staring intently. Another grizzly was watching the theft of the hive!

They were both males, and this made the event doubly interesting to Sandy Sweyn. He pressed himself close to the trunk of a tree and stood at gaze, perfectly confident that the two would presently be so absorbed in the doings of one another that he would not be heeded unless he actually shouted at their ears. For grizzly males do not meet in this fashion unless there is an excellent reason for it.

Therefore, he fairly gaped at the two. He who stood up at the bee tree was not the object of his quest. The formidable Buck was equipped with certain defects in the claws, with which Sandy was familiar. This fellow at the bee tree was a dark-robed giant with whose paws nothing whatever could be found at fault.

He, who squatted in the brush, therefore,

a dirty cream-gray in color, must be the cattle killer.

The honey seeker was now furiously at work with the heart of his problem. His powerful claws had already torn away bark and the outer and softer layers of the wood of that big tree. Although the core of the trunk was made of much sterner stuff, it, also, had to yield to the ripping claws and tearing teeth. Presently, his whole body shaking with terrible greed, the big dark-robed fellow pressed closer to the tree and began to wolf down the masses of honey.

Buck raised himself a little in the shadow of the trees. Behind the veil of the brush, Sandy could almost feel his envy at this wonderful feast.

The bees, swarming in brown-and-amber-flashing armies, made wild assaults upon the big bear, but all in vain. Whether they lighted on face or tangles, coat or paws, he paid no attention to the myriad of their stings but continued to gorge himself.

Only when the main mass of the honey had been consumed, he drew out his head from the tree and made a few careless passes with his paws to beat away some of the legions of infuriated honey makers.

There was more to be done in that nest. There were the grubs and the last remnants of the wax and honey to be devoured. As for the choice in delicacies, no grizzly would very well know how to choose between a bit of honey and the same weight of honey-fed grub.

So he at the tree paid no heed to the stealthy progress of Buck at his rear. Buck was moving like the best of hunters. A grizzly has not quite the uncanny ability of the moose to move through heavy brush without a sound; but still six or seven hundred pounds of bear will be maneuvered with wonderful silence through crackling underbrush. Buck, on mischief bent, and for revenge, slid on like a shadow among shadows.

He came out to the exact rear of this intruder upon his paws, and stole forward, foot by foot. Sandy shifted his place to gain a nearer view. When he was drawing nearer to the dark stranger one of the big feet of Buck snapped a small twig beneath him. Only the ghost of a sound, but it was enough to reach the electrically sensitive ears of the other even though they were partly muffled by the surrounding core of the tree. He jerked out his head.

However, Buck was instantly attacking. He leaped forward with a lightness wonderful in one of his bulk, reared, and struck like lightning with either forepaw. The weight of those blows would have torn the ribs out of a range bull; aimed at the head of the other grizzly, they knocked him flat.

He fell with a roll, however, and came to his feet as Buck rushed in to finish the fight with his teeth. Alas for too much eagerness! The dark-coated stranger was rearing as Buck rushed in, and the full weight of a driving forepaw landed on the snout of Sandy's quarry.

It was a solid stroke and stopped the charge of Buck as effectually as ever a well-aimed drive stopped a rushing pugilist in the ring. Buck, crumpling back on his hind quarters, came only half erect. Before he could gain his balance, the stranger was on him.

Nothing but the effect of the first surprise had enabled Buck to stand up to the other for even this length of time. If Buck, himself, had some six hundred pounds of durable weight and might, the stranger had a vital advantage of more than a hundred in weight. Besides, he was a good span of years younger. Youth had enabled him to recuperate quickly from the opening blows of his enemy. Youth now gave him the speed to lunge in, strangely like a human being, and grip the throat of Buck as the latter went down.

What a grip was there!

There is no bear that will not prefer infinitely to do his battles with the marvelous cunning and might of his forepaws. But when it comes to the finishing touches, he has jaws unmatched in the whole range of the American wilderness. A very admirable pair of jaws was now clamped in the throat of Buck.

He struggled as well as he could. It was only chance that gave him a moment's respite. One of the forepaws of the stranger came close to his own choking, gaping mouth, and instantly his great teeth were clamped upon it.

A roar of fury and pain — and the two were separated.

Once more they rushed together. Now a forepaw of the big dark bear dangled useless. He came off a bad second in the exchange of long-range blows, and so he pushed in close for the teeth again.

The weight of his lunge was too much for Buck again. Down he went; again the teeth of the stranger plunged into the throat.

Thirty seconds of writhing, gasping, and snarling; then the body of Buck quivered and lay still. Grinding deep through fur and flesh, the blunt canines of the conqueror had found the life nerve and destroyed it. Never again would Buck wander down toward the cattle ranges to eat his fill.

One tentative blow of his unwounded paw was tried by the victor. When Buck made no response, there were no further insults. The victor ambled slowly away, pausing to shake himself now and then, and limping heavily as his weight came rolling onto his badly bitten paw. Until, at length, that paw was lifted altogether, and the big chap went awkwardly off on three legs.

A moment later, Sandy Sweyn was busily at work on the job of skinning. First a long slit down the belly; and then one down each leg. After that followed a session of cutting and tugging. It is a hard task for two skillful men to take the robe from a big bear. In the mighty arms of Sandy Sweyn there resided a strength sufficient to do it all.

Three days later Peter Dunstan was at breakfast when he heard the voice of the cook roaring in the kitchen. "Here's Sandy back — and he's got it!"

"Got what? The bear?"

There stood Sandy in the doorway with a great pile of bearskin rolled upon his shoulder, a crushing weight of green hide.

"Good heavens, Sandy!" cried the rancher. "Have you carried that far?"

"Oh, about seventy-five miles," said Sandy Sweyn. "I thought that maybe you would like to have it."

# 8

Men west of the Rockies still place a very high value upon mere physical prowess. The result was that the roll of the bear's hide was weighed, green and heavy as it was, and when the poundage was known, two of Mr. Dunstan's punchers were commissioned to follow the trail of Sandy Sweyn through the lowlands and into the hills.

Even for horses, hard-ridden, that journey took nearly four days, though part of this was spent in worrying over the problems of the trail. When they returned to the ranch of Peter Dunstan, they came with the tale of a superman's achievement. As Shorty put it: "Not even a horse could of done that job and packed that hide back so fast!"

When the two came back, they found that trouble was in the air, for in the first place Mr. Dunstan had drawn from Sandy the true story of all that had happened in the little clearing among the pines. When he heard of the presence of a bear bigger and stronger than Buck, with a pelt twice as fine as the one which was now being cured, he was greatly excited.

He would have had Sandy Sweyn start at once in the pursuit of the second bear, but Sandy was strangely reluctant. When Dunstan pressed him, Sandy relapsed into a gloomy silence from which nothing at all could be gleaned.

In the meantime, however, Peter Dunstan had decided that Sandy must be handled with gloves. It was not that he was afflicted with any peculiar sympathy for Sandy, but rather because he now recognized in Sandy Sweyn a property of such value that the rancher began to feel that therein lay his most priceless single possession.

In a single season, such a matchless hunter as this might rid the Dunstan Range of all his coyotes, wolves, bears, and mountain lions. What would not this be worth to one who lost as many from his calf crop as did Peter Dunstan every year? Therefore, when Sandy Sweyn grew silent and morose, the rancher did not insist, but he said gloomily to the cook: "Now what the devil can be bothering him now?"

"I tell you," declared Steve McGuire, "that nobody is gunna get any good out of him. But he'll do more harm in the end than ever he done good. You write me down in red for that, partner!"

The rancher wrote him down in red, as a

97

matter of fact. He came to his new decision about the big invading grizzly. He would, himself, dispense with the services of Sandy and would ride up and try to trail the big fellow.

He informed Sandy to that effect. Sandy's reply was a staggerer to Mr. Dunstan. He sat with a contorted brow for a long time. Then he said:

"Look here, Mr. Dunstan, it ain't right, it seems to me."

"What's not right?"

"To kill that bear," said Sandy Sweyn.

"Not right to kill that bear?" shouted the rancher. "Why not, Sandy?"

"I dunno that the bear has harmed you, has he?" asked Sandy hopefully.

"Why, he's living on my land, part of the time, and he's apt to come down and begin to live on cattle the same way that Buck did, and kill hundred-dollar steers for the sake of one meal, the way that Buck did. Isn't that a harm to me?"

This proposition was long seriously considered by Sandy Sweyn. Finally he said:

"The way it seems to me — he is a bear, and no man."

"You're a wise fellow, Sandy," said the rancher ironically. "He's a bear and not a man. I grant you that."

"How could he know what pleases you and what don't please you? And was he *made* for the sake of pleasing you?"

"Maybe not," remarked the rancher, smiling with pity at this sort of logic. "But my rifle was not made for the sake of pleasing him, either."

This seemed a great point to Sandy Sweyn, and he went away and digested the thought for an hour. When he came back, he had attacked the problem from a new angle. He said to big Peter Dunstan: "If you was to knock down a man, would you hit him after he was down?"

"I suppose not."

"Well, that black grizzly has got a hurt forepaw. That paw is so bad hurt that he can't run very well to hide himself, and he can't very well manage to fight much for himself, either, can he?"

The patience of the rancher was ended. He exploded suddenly: "In the name of the devil, what are you talking about? What has this nonsense to do with my right to go out and shoot a bear on my own range — or a range right near to mine?"

The blank eyes of Sandy filled with trouble.

"It's this way," said he. "The trouble is that the black fellow — he was working for you and for me, in a way, when he killed

Buck, wasn't he?"

"Working for me?" shouted the rancher, infuriated and confused.

Sandy shrank back. Anger always bewildered and frightened him.

"You wanted Buck killed; and you sent me to do it. When the black fellow killed Buck, he did my work for me, and the thing that you wanted done. Ain't that all true?"

"By accident! By accident!" cried Peter Dunstan. "Do you think that a bear has a reasoning brain — or what *do* you think, Sandy?"

"I dunno," said Sandy, with a sigh. "Only, it seems to me that it ain't hardly right for the black fellow to be killed, like this."

"Bah!" exclaimed Peter Dunstan. "You stay here behind. I'm riding up through the hills with a couple of the boys. It's a long time since I've dropped a bear; but inside of a week, Sandy, you'll see the hide of the big black boy stretched out yonder beside that of Buck."

He picked out Shorty and "Doc" Lawrence, his two best trailers and surest shots. In their company he left the ranch that same afternoon.

They struck away merrily in the indicated direction, and all went so well that, the next morning, they were well into the uplands. That very evening, cutting in great circles for sign, they came upon the trail of the mighty stranger who limped with one forepaw, stepping constantly short with it. On that trail they gathered. All through the day it grew clearer and clearer before them, until they discovered, in the mid-afternoon, that another horseman was riding on the same trail! For the sign of his horse lay before them, wherever the ground was soft enough to show the impression of his hoofs.

They pressed on more eagerly than ever, but now they came to country so rough that the horses had to be abandoned to the care of Doc while Shorty and Peter Dunstan, being expert mountaineers, went forward with rifles and small knapsacks.

In the rougher going, even with a wounded paw, the bear could make better time comparatively. Still they felt sure that no crippled beast could long keep away from them. They pressed on swiftly, steadily, drawing their belts tighter as the day grew older. In the gold of the late afternoon, Shorty pointed with a sudden shout. The rancher looked up, too late to see.

"The bear?" he cried.

"No, but a hoss and man — a sort of a blue-looking hoss — it must be the gent that's hunting the bear ahead of us!"

The hoofprints, which had disappeared as

the rough going began, now started in once more. Though it seemed a miracle that horse and rider could make any time over such going. "Unless that hoss has got a cross strain of mountain sheep in him!" said Shorty.

All through the rest of the afternoon, they drew fresher and fresher upon the spore. At the very end of the day they came to a crushing disappointment. The bear had crossed a natural bridge which spanned a narrow gorge. Then, turning, he must have ripped the top boulders away until he came to the keystone of the arch. In the bottom of the gorge lay the rubble of fallen stones; in front of the two hunters there was a dismal gap of twenty feet — more than either of them cared to risk by jumping.

"I've heard of wise bears and wise bears!" muttered Peter Dunstan, "but never of one like this lame devil, and I'm going to get him now or die trying. Why, Shorty, this bear is worth writing a book about, if he has the sense to do tricks like this!"

Shorty shook his head solemnly.

"Chief," said he, "no bear ever broke down that bridge. It was done by the gent that's riding ahead of us. He broke it down so that we couldn't get at the bear before him."

"Man, man!" cried the rancher, pointing to the junk heap of immense stones in the bottom of the ravine. "Is there any man you know of that could handle stones the size of them?"

"Aye," said Shorty, coloring a little. "There's one man. You know him, too!"

It was true that Mr. Dunstan understood the meaning of Shorty perfectly, but he made no reference to his understanding. He merely gave his strength and agility and patience to climbing down the near wall of the ravine and ascending upon the farther side. This work consumed an hour's time and left them utterly spent. As they came to the edge of the cliff, on the farther side of the ravine, they heard the ringing report of a rifle before them.

"The young devil!" murmured Peter Dunstan. "He wouldn't let me kill that bear with my own gun — he had to — And now we'll meet him coming back, carrying the hide!"

They built a large fire to direct the lucky hunter ahead of them. No Sandy Sweyn appeared.

The next morning they had not advanced a half mile on their way along the trail before they came upon a half-consumed carcass of a mountain sheep. It had been shot from the towering rocks above and had broken its bones to bits in the fall from the height. It had not been more than touched by the hunter. Around the body were the huge imprints of the feet of the bear that they had been hunting so eagerly. It had evidently dined most heartily.

Peter Dunstan swore volubly. He avoided the eye of Shorty as they hurried on down the trail again, for each knew the thought of the other, and each felt that that thought was too ridiculous to be trusted in words.

Presently they came to a line of blazes; that thickly blazed trail led them to a tree from which a great section of the face had been chopped away, leaving a broad and very fairly smooth white surface upon which certain letters had been inscribed in a great, painful, childishly sprawling hand:

*I don't think that you should worry this bear no more. He ain't troubled you none.*

"It's Sandy!" said the rancher. "And you were right, Shorty. But it's a hard thing to believe that a man would ride up here for the sake of working for a bear!"

Shorty shook his head.

"This Sandy Sweyn, he's different," said he. "I seen that when I seen the way that he rode on that roan mare. Because I could tell that he knew how to lighten his weight a whole lot. No, he's a pretty queer sort of a man, chief. I tell you, right now he's riding his hoss right alongside of that bear — otherwise, his tracks would fall in a straight line right on top of the grizzly's tracks."

This conjecture might be wild, but at least, there was the token upon the ground, as they crossed a bit of soft mountain turf, where the imprints were clearly revealed. There was the trail of the bear and just beside it the more deeply driven hoofmarks of the horse.

"It ain't natural, and it ain't right — but it's a fact!" said Shorty. "And there you can see it with your own eyes."

Peter Dunstan stopped and swore a great oath.

"I'm going to keep right after this trail," said he, "if it takes me the rest of my life. I'm going to have that bear's hide and claws. Do you hear me, Shorty?"

"I'd rather not, though," said Shorty, "because I've got an idea that maybe you'll wish that you hadn't said that same thing!"

They hurried on again, striding long and free.

"Because," said big Peter Dunstan, "you can see how it is. That bear doesn't have to stop to forage for himself. He's got a hunter with him, and that hunter kills his game for him. As for his lame paw — why, he seems to be able to bear up on that, well enough!"

For these reasons, they worked fast and gave themselves no rest. The evening of the next day found them footsore, utterly exhausted, and very hungry. Just at the setting of the sun, they came upon a crooked pine tree on the side of the hill, with the face cut away as the other tree had been. Upon the white surface thus exposed there was written in that same labored and sprawling hand:

*This bear can't go no farther, but I ain't gunna let you come at him.*
                                    *Sandy Sweyn.*

"He's not going to *let* us?" said Peter Dunstan. "Does the fool mean that he would actually —"

The next morning, when he prepared to start out on the trail, Shorty remained stubbornly in the camp.

"Look here," said he. "I ain't a coward, I hope. But I ain't gunna get myself killed for the sake of any bear that was ever born. I don't value them hides so much as all of that, y'understand? And this Sandy Sweyn, he means business, now. When he means business, he shoots too straight to please me a little bit. I'm gunna stay right put here in the camp. You go ahead if you want to. I'll start out a little later and make myself a burying party!"

Peter Dunstan was angered by this defection. But after all, Shorty was a proved man of worth. The rancher had to start on by himself, in a towering passion. Passion was not great enough in him to make him go without caution. He stole through the scattering forest of these highlands with all the skill which he could muster. He came, at length, to a region of bare rocks, with a stream trickling feebly down among them — a region where there was cover, to be sure, but not cover like that of the woods.

Pausing, Peter Dunstan looked to the loading of his rifle. For the first time in his life, big Peter Dunstan went out actually on the man trail. He had worked his way for a scant fifty yards when something whistling and wickedly brief passed above his head. It was a sound heard and gone before he could be sure that it was approaching. He jerked up his head in haste and snatched his rifle to his shoulder.

There was nothing before him, but a bullet had just been fired over his head! Yet Peter Dunstan went slowly on, for he was a very brave man, and shame and anger were forcing him along, as well as a great reputation which needed to be upheld.

Thirty slow yards away he found the following charcoal legend scraped upon the face of a rock:

*Dear Mr. Dunstan: I ain't gunna kill you unless you make me.*

*Sandy Sweyn.*

Peter Dunstan felt the cold perspiration roll down his forehead. He realized, now, that that bullet had not been an accidental miss. It had been merely a warning: the next one fired by this hidden marksman would certainly put a period to his life.

He did not hesitate an instant. He stood up, turned his back upon the forward trail and all the oaths which he had sworn to keep to it. He trudged slowly, with bent head, back to the fire where Shorty sat, quietly smoking.

Shorty stood up and nodded.

"I knew that you'd use good sense, chief," said he.

His chief made no reply. They went slowly on the back trail toward the far distant point where they had left Doc with the horses. All through that day, hardly a word was spoken, man to man, except a monosyllable, here and there. When the darkness came, Peter Dunstan dropped a buck, as it sprang from a little covert. That night the roasted venison loosened their tongues.

"Two miracles," said Dunstan. "How could he ride a horse through country like this? Second miracle — how could he tame that bear

108

enough to travel with it — even granting that he's crazy enough to really want to save the bear — and not just to make me mad?"

"I dunno," said Shorty. "But I sort of wish, chief, that you hadn't drove him off into the hills like this."

"Drove him off?" shouted the rancher. "What are you talking about?"

"Man, man," said Shorty with the dignity of the self-assured, "didn't he bring you in the bearskin that you wanted? Why shouldn't you let a poor half-wit like him keep the other bear where it was till it got well — and then he would of gone out and killed that bear for you his own self — or led you right up where you could of got in your shot at it!"

Peter Dunstan, for some reason, could not answer. He felt that half of his reputation had been torn from him, however. He suddenly found himself echoing the words of Steve McGuire:

"Nobody will ever gain, in the end, by anything that this fellow Sandy Sweyn might do. He's nothing but bad luck, Shorty."

Shorty said after a time:

"We're gunna hear a lot more about him, chief, since he's up here in the mountains. Suppose that some gents meet up with him that see that he's a half-wit and don't see that he's what we know — a gent with a murder in each of his hands, if he wants to use them! There's apt to be dead men in these parts, chief. And I hope that you ain't gunna be blamed for them!"

Once again, Peter Dunstan had nothing to say. There was nothing remaining for him to do except to ride back to his ranch and there face the old life with the new name and the bad name which he had made for himself. He cursed the day when his eyes first fell on the blank eyes of Sandy Sweyn. Something told Peter Dunstan that the days of his strength and the days of his glory were nearly at an end. This was a foretaste of his fall.

As for Sandy Sweyn — no one saw him for a long time. But there was a wild tale repeated some time later in the mountain villages about a great, dark-coated grizzly bear who was seen at close hand, with what appeared to be a cloth bandage wrapped around a forepaw. In the rear, behind the monster, followed a man. The wind blew from that shadowy form of a man to the bear, and yet the bear's hair-trigger nostrils gave it no warning — or else this one man of all the race it did not fear.

# 9

*"Palabras de Boca, piedras de honda,"* said Diego Mirandos, who was fond, like most Mexicans, of bringing in a pat proverb wherever the chance offered. He said this at a time when chance so framed affairs that never was a proverb more truly applied.

"Words of the mouth, stones of the sling," Diego Mirandos had said, and quite truly for, after all, words fly as far and strike as deep as stones from a sling. To the truth of this remark pretty Catalina Mirandos could not be expected to pay any heed. She was in a mighty passion. Standing on the veranda of the house, she looked across the garden which her own hands had helped to make beautiful in this strange land of the Americans; then she twisted her fingers together and shook her head in violence.

José Rezan stood before her. He was at the bottom of the steps, but he was so big, and she was so small that even at that disadvantage he seemed nearly as tall as she. He was Mexican as much as she. Yet some said that his was a Russian name. Certainly his hair was blond, and his skin was pale.

He had said: "I have ridden everywhere. I have searched everywhere. But the little devil of a horse — I cannot find her, Catalina. She has turned herself into a mist, and she has disappeared."

Poor José! He was so big, so strong, so calm in his bigness and in his strength, that he loved her all the more because she was so tremendously spoiled. Her father was a big man and a gentle one also. For so many years he had poured out to Catalina all that her heart could desire that it had grown impossible for her to endure a disappointment.

"I'll get her for you if I can, Catalina," said big José. "But you have to remember that we trapped her by accident really. She was always more than half wild — a real little devil, dear Catalina."

"Do not call me dear! I am not dear — I am not yours!"

The eyes of José Rezan grew greater than ever with a sudden fear.

"Consider, Catalina, that she will have gone back to the same wild herd from which she came, perhaps. But even if it took hundreds of dollars, I shall send men to follow her and run her down, and catch her if they can."

"Run her down, starve her down, ruin her, break her spirit!" cried Catalina. "Do I want a diamond with the fire gone from it? No, no, no! I shall have my Elena — my Elena Blanca — my beautiful white one! I shall have her again. I shall have her without a hair changed. I shall see her just as she was. And if there is so much as a rope scald on one of her legs, I will not take her at all. I will not, I will not!"

José was paler than ever. His eyes rolled frantically from side to side, seeking for help. Finding nothing that could save him, he said: "It is only three days to the wedding. After we are married a little time, Catalina, I shall go myself —"

"*After* we are married?" screamed the little tyrant. "No, but before! Before!"

"Ah, my dear," said José, "but can I catch Elena Blanca and bring her back to you all in three short days? Can I do that?"

"Three days or thirty days!" said Catalina Mirandos. "What do I care? I love Elena Blanca. I must have her again. And I shall never marry any but the man who brings her back to me!"

José Rezan struck his big hands together.

"Child, child — you must not say it. You have given me your word, and the priest knows it!"

"I take my word back. I catch it back!" cried Catalina Mirandos. "I catch it back and keep it again and swear a new oath!"

"Catalina, you kill me with sorrow!"

"Ah, but you do not care when *I* die! You do not care at all. It is only for your own huge self that you care! I lose my beautiful Elena, and it is nothing to you. My father has told you to kill her, or to give her away, or to turn her loose — and you have done it!"

"I swear —"

"Do not be perjured! I would not believe your oath. But I swear —" Here a sudden and a heavy voice struck in from the side, the voice of her father, Diego Mirandos:

"Do not swear, Catalina!"

But she cried shrilly at them nevertheless: "I swear that I shall never marry, except the man that brings Elena Blanca back to me!"

Poor José Rezan! He shrank from her, and a thousand terrible possibilities rushed upon his mind. It was at this moment that her father said solemnly:

*"Palabras de boca, piedras de honda!"*

With that solemn voice ringing in her ear, even little Catalina Mirandos understood, indeed, that the word she had spoken might be like the stones from a sling. Where would they fall; whom would they strike? Or might they not return upon her?

Then, for fear lest they should see the terror

114

in her eyes, she whirled around, raced into the house, and got to her room where the silks whispered and rustled about her, and the canary began suddenly to sing for joy at the sight of her. There she lay, curled up on a couch, and felt the beating of her heart that made all her body quiver, while she said to herself over and over:

"Surely it cannot be such a terrible thing that I have said! What difference can they make — the words that poor little Catalina may speak?"

A minute later she had nearly forgotten that last scene, except for a guilty sense of pleasure because of the pain that she had given to big, honest José and to her father, Don Diego. After that, she was thinking of nothing but Elena Blanca once more, yearning for her.

You must consider that, in all the world of horses, there was only one made for Catalina. That was the white mare. She had been a bright vision of delight, enchanting the eyes of many a hunter and many a cowpuncher who had some dazzling glimpse of her as she fled away across the hills or stood like a frightened deer against a dark bank of the pine trees.

Chance brought her into the hands of José, who gave her into the hands of the lady of his heart. With infinite labor, through weeks and weeks, that wild creature was tamed until

Catalina could be trusted in the saddle on her back. It was a crimson saddle, all fretted over with silver, and there was a crimson bridle worked with shining gold. When they saw the little mare dance forth, they knew that all their work had been well rewarded. It was like a harmony of well-matched sounds, seeing the beauty of the girl and the beauty of Elena Blanca together.

As for Catalina, she knew that when she sat on the back of White Helen she was mounted, as it were, upon an enchanted horse, with the surety that she could ride forthright into the hearts of all men. Do you wonder that she should have cared so much about this — seeing that she was betrothed to marry the good José, so rich, so handsome and so strong? You wonder, only because you did not know Catalina.

Perhaps the wild oath which Catalina had spoken that day would never have been heard of again had it not been that another ear had listened, the ear of Rosa, the half-breed *moza*. In another moment she was at the stable door, whispering to her wild-faced son, Filipo:

"The kind God has prepared riches and happiness for you, son. The señorita has sworn that she will marry only the man who brings back the white mare. Whose hand but yours tamed her and trained her? And who but you

116

will find her trail and catch her again?"

"An oath is only a word," said Filipo, trembling at the thought of all that might be.

"Oh, fool, fool!" gasped out Rosa. "It is the oath of a Mirandos, and their word is sacred always!"

Filipo did not wait. He started at once, on his fastest pony, with his best rawhide lariat coiled beside the saddle. There was fire in his heart, and the thought of the señorita was like a living breath from heaven. He rode straight through the village down the trail. It was only when he got to the farther side that he remembered a certain little house on the edge of the town where, for a certain price, a known man might buy forbidden liquor, and drink it in a circle of the discreet.

He turned back and sat in the little house the rest of that day. By the time that the evening came, there were others around him. The spirit of good fellowship carried the heart of Filipo upon the wings of a swallow. He was in such a heaven of content that it seemed a bitter wrong that the precious secret should remain in his hands, only.

Therefore, he confided it to one, and then to another. Before the world was an hour older, the eavesdropping vixen, Rumor, had seized on the tidings and was abroad — clattering out the story.

Before the next morning, every soul in the village had heard. Before the next sunset, the word was gone across the mountains, running like liquid fire down every valley, from village to village, from ranch to ranch.

There is nothing like competition to create excitement. If the challenge had gone out to catch the white mare alone, it would have brought a great answer. When such a reward as the hand of the Mexican girl was added, there was hardly a cowpuncher, competent or incompetent, who did not raise his head.

The newspaper got hold of the thing quickly enough. Half a dozen photographers slipped out to the house of Don Diego, and managed to get snapshots of the beauty before her father herded them away, promising that the next man to approach the place with such an infernal machine should have a thorough slating down with lead, placed in the spots where it would do the most good.

However, the mischief had been done much too thoroughly to be undone. There was the story, in the first place, which editors caught up on the run and printed in broad columns, under titles sometimes witty, and sometimes not. Afterward, when the pictures went the rounds, the tale was printed again, with many embroideries.

It was something more than the melodramatic hunger of a pretty girl for publicity. Every one knew that the tale had gone abroad by accident. In addition, when the house and the lands of Don Diego were described, even the most conservative could tell that in this game there was something of greater value than the mere pictures on the cards. Besides, a girl might have been offered for any other prize in the whole world and been considered either vain-glorious or a fool.

When she offered herself in exchange for the return of her horse — why, that was a different matter, by far, you may be sure. It touched the romantic sense of irresponsibility which runs in every human being, especially in every Westerner.

The pictures crowned it all. Those wicked photographers had been trained to their arts in devious ways. They had practiced, themselves, according to their politics, in snapping the candidate for mayor and making him look like a jackass; or in snapping him to make him appear a philosopher and a philanthropist. They had been able to make old actresses appear to be young ones; they had learned the secret of putting guilt or innocence upon the faces of accused men.

When it merely came to showing the grace and beauty of Catalina Mirandos, they were at their ease. They showed her swinging into the saddle on another horse, stepping from the door of the house, in the garden, startled and letting an armful of flowers drop to the ground.

The editors, rubbing their hands, printed the pictures one by one. On each day, in some manner, to justify the successive stories, they raked up new material — something about Diego Mirandos and the angle of Mexican politics which had made him move north of the Rio Grande; or something about the famous white mare, which had been sighted and run her, and only sighted there — or something.

Best of all, were the stories about the girl herself, this last entirely out of the imaginations of the editors. They really agreed upon one point only — which was that the lovely girl was the only human being in all the world who could ride the spirited mare. That to her touch the strength and fire of White Helen responded instantly, and she became as a lamb.

On the whole, it was what even a metropolitan paper, in the daily hunt for "human interest," would have accepted with open arms and open columns.

As for the thousands of strong men who were at all near to the region through which the mare was wandering, those who were unmarried saddled their best horses, and those who were married looked down impatiently and scowled at the left hands of their wives.

To no one did the sight of the girl's picture come with a greater shock than to Peter Dunstan, whose ranch during the last years, had spread wider and wider, eating up the adjoining cattle places.

It struck him like the surprise of a midnight attack. A sudden rush, a whispering of many rapid feet — and then the voices of triumph are sounding over the great fortress before it is well roused from the drowsy content of its impregnability.

So it was with Peter Dunstan.

He formed his plan on the spot. The others had failed in spite of the numbers which they had employed — like the rich lumberman from Montana, who had come down with twenty men and whole trains of fleet horses to capture the white mare.

Peter Dunstan did not intend to work with numbers. He intended to use only one person. That was one whose skill was without a duplicate in all the world.

# 10

He took with him, of all of his band of hard riders and trained punchers, only the redoubtable retainer. Shorty.

They rode north. They crossed the belt of the sun-scorched desert. They crossed the region of the scrub cedar and futile lodge-pole pines. They rode on north, where the trees grew thicker and bigger. Then they entered upon a region of plentiful rainfall.

Here they began to make their inquiries.

Shorty said, scratching his red head, "This here is the sort of a country that you'll be sure to find him in. There ain't any doubt but that he likes a country where there's trees and water, because in them parts he'll find the animals."

"And the birds," said Peter Dunstan.

Shorty turned sharply about in the saddle and peered at his companion. "Birds," said he, in a gasping voice, "birds, too?"

"Birds, too," said Peter Dunstan, with the calm of superior knowledge.

"Aye," said Shorty, after he had considered this tiding for a time. "Anything that ain't got human speech, I suppose!"

So they came to a little crossroads town, and Shorty asked the blacksmith, who sat upon his rusting anvil, if there had been any sight in that region of a man who rode a blue horse and lived in the woods.

"A blue horse?" said the blacksmith. "Might you have been drinking, partner?"

"All right," said Shorty to his chief, not deigning to answer this remark. "He ain't been around here!"

They journeyed on, a wild, rough way, sometimes finding a ranch house or a little town to stay in at night, sometimes never coming to shelter, but sleeping out in the raw mountain winds, with the naked stars close and bright above their heads. Wherever they went, they asked the same question: "Have you seen a gent around these parts, riding on a blue horse? A blue mare?"

Everywhere, they were met with gaping mouths and staring eyes and no information.

"But," said Peter Dunstan, "it begins to seem to me that we'll never find him. He may have had the claws of a mountain lion ripping through his inwards before this, Shorty!"

"Him?" said Shorty. "Nope, he ain't the kind that'll ever die by no wild animal. No varmint will ever sink a tooth into him, I guess."

They came, in the bleak evening of a windy day, with the gale whipping volleys of rain against the roofs, upon the sight of the little village where a stream of lumber wagons crossed another stream of wagons from the nearest silver mine. The village had come into existence as a way station and a depot, where supplies for the neighboring ranchers could be stored. Into this straggling place they rode, putting up at the one-story hotel.

Because they were tired, and because they were beginning to despair of success, they delayed their inquiries until supper had been finished. Then Peter Dunstan said, as usual:

"Have any of you fellows seen a man riding a blue horse in these parts?"

There was the usual blank silence, but before the voices of wonder could break in and ask what was meant, a man said sharply from the foot of his table, lowering his coffee cup with a click:

"What might *you* know about a gent with a blue hoss?"

"I'm asking you if he's been seen," said Peter Dunstan.

"Might you be a friend of his?" asked the other, with gathering wrath masked under a gentle voice.

"No," said Dunstan truthfully enough.

"Well," said the other, letting his anger

break through restraint, "next to layin' my hands on that ornery, good-for-nothin' sneak, I'd like nothin' better than to get hold of any friend of his and bust him in two and see what there is so funny on the insides of him."

"I see," said Dunstan, nodding, "that you know the man that I'm after!"

Early the next morning, they took to the saddle and were soon on their way. That day and the next, till nearly noon, they traveled, until they came to the crest of a narrow range of mountains. Still north and west from this, they looked down upon a wide sweep of forest, cut by the shining length of many a stream. Here, there was a pool, and there, a long and narrow lake. Trees were everywhere, only falling back now and again, from some patch of bright green meadow, set like a jewel among the shadows of the trees — the field of grass which had grown up around the site of some vanished lake.

All of this, small with distance and clear under the noonday sun, they could see as distinctly as though they had taken a fine picture and held it at arm's length.

"It's the right place," said Shorty with emphasis.

"You talk as sure," said Peter Dunstan, "as though you knew what was going on inside of the head of the kid, Shorty. What makes you so almighty confident that you're right?"

"I'll tell you," said Shorty. "Right from the very first, I've had an idea that I could feel something of what he was thinking. That day that he beat me, riding the roan hoss and me carrying your money — well, right on that day, it seemed to me that as he come whizzing up behind me, gaining every jump, I could feel a sort of *pity* coming out of his mind, y'understand? Like he hardly wanted to beat me, because I was riding so hard. And when he come by me, dog-gone if I wasn't right, because he was looking across at me and shaking his head. That was when he was rounding the rock at the end of the run."

"Well," said the rancher, "if you can guess what goes on inside of his head, you beat me, Shorty. But you were always a sort of queer one yourself. How d'you think that we can go about catching this wild man, now that we've come to the place."

"This is the right place," said Shorty. "And you can lay to that! What more would he like? Here's plenty of water for him to do his fishing in. And here's plenty of trees. There'll be bear and beaver, and bees and bugs and birds, too, since you say that he likes them. Them waters have got kingfishers and fish hawks hangin' over them, you can bet. And if them cliffs across the way ain't got a few nests of eagles on them, I'm a fool.

"Yes, sir, this is the place for him. And most of all because there ain't any houses near. No houses between this here range and the next, so far as I can see. Nothing but a tangle of trees and creeks, and what not. This trail ain't been worn none too smooth!"

So ended Shorty, and his master looked at him with a touch of awe; it was not the first time that he had had to look at the little cow-puncher in this fashion. He allowed Shorty to lead the way as, instead of dipping down into this unknown region, they wound along the side of the ridge, and so across to more open cattle country, with a tiny huddle of houses in the distance — a range town which they reached in the dusk.

"Now what?" asked the rancher.

"When you go fishing," said Shorty, "you find a likely looking stream and then you get a hook, and then you get your bait. Yonder is the sort of a place that the fish, we want, would like. And you and me are the hook. Now you go to get us the bait."

"Bait!" echoed Peter Dunstan.

"Yes," said Shorty. "What is the most noise-makingest thing that there is, on four feet?"

"A calf," said the rancher.

Shorty shook his head.

"I got to admit," said he, "that when a calf wants its maw, it gets to working a fine pair of lungs, but you take it at a little distance, and the bawling of a calf sort of melts into things in general. It ain't hardly no more than the roar of a waterfall, as you might say. What we want, is a noise that'll travel through your ears right down to your backbone!"

The rancher nodded.

"I've got the thing for you," said he. "A dog. Not a grown dog, nor yet a little puppy, but one about six months old, used to one home. Put that in a strange place, and it'll make a noise nobody within five miles can sleep through."

"You got your uses, Dunstan," said the cowpuncher, grinning. "Now and then, the things that you think of come in pretty handy, I got to admit. But now the next thing that I want is to find that same pup."

They found it readily at hand. In the very hotel where they stopped was a happy family of sheep dogs. A mother and four puppies not five months old — all legs and clumsiness, but with bright, warm eyes that told of growing mischief and wisdom, hand in hand.

Two dollars made the purchase. The next morning, Shorty was busy at the blacksmith's.

"I want a collar," said he, "that can't be broke. An iron collar forged right so it'll fit the neck of this here dog, partner. One made out of a good kind of steel, that nothing but a steel saw or a good file will get through — and that none too quick. Y'understand? Then I want a chain of the same style. A chain strong enough to hold a hoss, friend!"

The thing was done, and no questions asked. In the West, strangeness in a stranger is taken for granted. The collar was made, and the chain was linked to it.

With the collar on the dog, and the chain fastened into the ring of the collar, the two men started on their ride.

It was not a pleasant ride. For whoever has taken an untrained puppy away from his old home will understand that noise is the element by which they live.

All this while, though he understood nothing of all of these preparations, Mr. Dunstan said not a word. Due to his wonder, his admiration for Shorty rose with every step of the journey.

They continued straight on into the woods until they reached a narrow clearing, with the glint of the nearest brook shining at them through the trunks of the trees. There Shorty made halt.

It was near the evening of the day. At once he fastened the dog to the trunk of a strong tree, hammering down the locking link with a heavy stone until it would have taken a cold chisel to pry it open again. After that, they retired — but not unaccompanied. The wild wailings of the dog followed them until Peter Dunstan wanted to hurry on, and leave the sound far sunk from hearing behind them.

Shorty would not hurry. He stopped in the very first shelter, sitting down to smoke a cigarette, while the horses cropped the grass, or jerked up their heads to listen to new notes in the crying of the dog.

"Suppose," said Peter Dunstan, "that something comes along and takes a notion to have dog meat for dinner?"

"We got to chance it," said Shorty.

"Besides," said Dunstan, "what the devil good can you get out of —"

He stopped. The last cry of the dog had turned into an almost human scream of pain and of terror. Then there was heavy silence. Even the horses understood and crowded closer together.

The two men rode back, as fast as the crowding trees would permit them to go. When they came to the spot they found only a splotch of crimson on the collar and a dabbling on the chain. The dog had been torn away and carried off. On an open, naked patch of forest mold, there was the vast imprint of a mountain lion's foot.

Peter Dunstan did not shudder, but his upper lip curled.

"This is the devil, Shorty!" said he. "Why did you do it, man?"

"I'm going back for another of the pups in the morning," said Shorty. "Can you stand it?"

"Get me the kid," said Peter Dunstan, "and you can kill half the dogs in the world! But it sort of leaves a stain on the whole business."

"Well," said Shorty, "this ain't my party; it's yours."

Which, after all, was true. Not a word of objection came from Peter Dunstan when his cowpuncher rode back toward the village in the early dawn of the next day. Not a word of protest came from him when the puppy was staked out in another clearing, deeper within the forest.

Once more the two men retired. This time, they passed only the nearest fringe of the forest and then paused to wait for results.

# 11

The wailing of that sheep dog was a terrible thing. It rose and died and rose again, soaring across the evening and the forest. Shorty shuddered, but Peter Dunstan, having once resigned himself to the necessity of the cruelty, paid not the slightest heed to the agony in that puppy's voice.

Then, far through the woods, they heard the long note of a mountain lion — no doubt the same which had answered the cry of the dog on the evening before and found a dainty titbit waiting on the chain, helpless to flee away. The note came again, nearer, and so pitched was the hunting voice of the great beast of prey that the men could not be sure from which direction it floated toward them. A fugitive from the voice of terror might as well have run into the mouth of the danger as fled away from it.

Said Shorty: "I'll get closer and take a shot at the varmint, if he shows himself."

"Sit still," said Peter Dunstan. "A dog is only a dog. I don't know what you intend to gain for me by letting the pup howl. But after all, a dog is only a dog."

Shorty had to sit still and contain himself, with a mighty effort, while the voice of the hunter sounded again, close at hand. Apparently there was not long lease of life for the puppy, and the last cry of the puma brought a wild lament from the sheep dog. Shorty clapped his hands over his ears. At that very moment a gun cracked in the trees near by; the death yell of the puma followed. Shorty leaped up and gripped the shoulder of his companion in the greatest excitement.

"It's him!" said Shorty. "I knew that I'd fetch him if he was in hearing of the yapping of that pup. It's him! Now, Dunstan, if you want him, you get close enough to see him catch that dog!"

Peter Dunstan's turn had come to shiver with excitement. He slipped to the edge of the little clearing on the farther side of which the dog was tethered. Crouching there in the shadows, he waited, his eyes accustomed to the dim light and probing the darkness alertly.

There was unbroken silence. The sheep dog, wearied out, or as though knowing that the sound of the gun and the death cry of the mountain lion signified the approach of a friend, stood motionless, erect, head high, with only a slight wagging of his tail in a pleasurable anticipation.

Though Peter Dunstan was an old hunter and a good one, yet he heard not a whisper of approach. He did not have the slightest idea that another person was near him until the puppy broke into a frantic whine of delight. Then Dunstan saw the youngster throwing himself in wild joy on the shadow of a man that emerged from the woods.

A dim and furtive shadow of a man it was. With a mere gesture — or at least Dunstan could hear no voice — this stealthy stranger reduced the dog to silence. The soft clinking of the chain told that the man was working to release the puppy.

Now, Peter Dunstan had done his share of fighting in his time, but it seemed to him that the danger of stepping forth into that clearing was greater than the danger of facing any leveled gun. He even thought of covering the other with his rifle before he ventured forth.

This he could not decide upon. For in that faint light in the woods, it seemed to Dunstan that he would be facing hopeless odds if the other should attempt to attack him. It would be like facing a royal tiger, felt Dunstan, a tiger which uses a gun and sees in the dark.

So he merely called out:

"Sandy! Sandy Sweyn!"

The form of the man vanished. Perhaps it was a backward leap into the surrounding trees that whisked him from sight. But the thing happened so suddenly and so noiselessly that the blood rushed into the head of Peter Dunstan; it was as though he had looked upon a miracle.

He stepped out into the open. There was no rustling among the brush, but he *felt* the withdrawal of the other to a greater distance, a swift and smooth withdrawal.

"Sandy," he called frantically. "Sandy, I mean you no harm. I swear I mean you no harm, Sandy."

Still, though he heard nothing, he felt the withdrawal of the other.

"Sandy, Sandy!" he called. "Come back, Sandy, and you'll have something worthwhile!"

There was a pause, and Peter Dunstan, cursing softly to himself, stared about into the shadows. The sheep dog made a tentative step forward, and then strained frantically in the direction in which the stranger had disappeared. Peter Dunstan cursed the dog and its whining. With the oath still on his lips, he looked up, and he was aware of the shadow of a man, standing just within the trees.

He took heart again, and said in his most amiable tones: "Are you there, Sandy?"

"I s'pose that I'm here," answered Sandy Sweyn. "And what might you want?"

"I want a word with you, Sandy!"

"Is that your dog?" asked Sandy suddenly.

"Yes," said Dunstan.

"I would make you a trade," said Sandy Sweyn.

"A trade?" said Dunstan, seizing upon the first opportunity to open up the conversation. "Why, son, what is it that you want, that I have?"

"Yonder," said Sweyn, "there is a lion lyin' dead. I would give you the skin of that, Mr. Dunstan."

"Why, man, that's kind of you. What do you want to trade it for?"

"That dog, Mr. Dunstan. I have sort of taken a hankering after that dog. Would you make the trade. Hist, boy!"

The sheep dog had begun to leap frantically toward the man in the shadows, but the soft hiss of Sandy Sweyn made the puppy drop to the ground and lie there, motionless; waiting and watching the new master.

There was something in the dog that made the man come slowly, stealthily forth. He was walking over dried leaves and twigs, it seemed to Peter Dunstan, and yet this uncanny forester moved without a sound. He came closer to the puppy and stretched a hand toward him. That youngster instantly was up, mute with the greatness of its joy, licking the fingers of

Sandy Sweyn. Peter Dunstan saw that he had a great power placed in his hands.

Just why any man should yearn after a dog like this — too young and untrained to be of vital use — was a great mystery to Peter Dunstan. He himself would not have given five dollars for half a dozen such creatures. But be that as it may, it was certain that the cunning of Shorty had devised a bait for Sandy Sweyn which had not only brought the strange fellow to hand, but which was still drawing him.

Dunstan said: "Why, Sandy, I don't want to disappoint you. I'd *like* to give you what you want. But this dog you understand how a man will come to love a dog, Sandy, even when he hasn't had him very long?"

He could see the head of Sandy nodding. That was just the sort of a thing which the odd brain of Sandy *could* comprehend.

"Aye," said Sandy, "I can see what you mean. And if I got to love a thing, well, I couldn't hardly give it up, I suppose!"

"But," said Peter Dunstan, "we might as well sit down and talk the thing over. I have in mind another sort of a trade, Sandy. I would like to trade a horse for that dog!"

Sandy started.

"You mean that I'm to trade Cleo for the dog?" said he, with a sort of horror.

"Trade in the blue mare?" asked big Peter Dunstan, laughing. "Oh, no. The horse that I want is a little thing. She would never carry your weight, Sandy, for half a day. A pretty thing, though. A little white mare."

"How would I buy her, though?"

"Not buy her, but catch her, because she's running wild."

"Ah," said Sandy, with a sigh of relief, "that's a different sort of a thing. I guess that maybe we could manage that."

"Good, Sandy! I'm very glad that you see the point that I'm making. You get the dog, you see, to keep as long as he lives. And then you get me the little mare."

"But how big might she be?"

"Oh, a little thing. An inch, or maybe two inches under fifteen hands."

"Aye," said Sandy. "I would not be wanting her, I suppose. And where might she be found?"

"I'll tell you all about that. Shall we sit down and talk it over?"

He struck a match as he spoke, touched it to a bunch of grass at his feet and scattered a handful of twigs over it. From that small beginning, the flame spread in another moment to a comfortable fire. Then Sandy Sweyn sat down beside his companion, on a log.

"Now," said Peter Dunstan, "I may as well

tell you that other men are hunting for this same mare."

"Ah, yes," said Sandy Sweyn. "And yet they haven't caught her?"

"They haven't caught her. She is as fast as a streak of lightning. Faster, I suppose, than any horse on the range."

"Faster than Cleo?" asked Sweyn, in surprise.

"Faster than Cleo — when Cleo has to carry your weight on her back, I presume."

"Well, I'll have to find that out for myself. How far away is the place where she is running?"

"Out on the Condon Desert. Do you know that country?"

"I don't know it. How far?"

"Oh, a hundred miles from here."

"And if I catch the mare?"

"You bring her to me, Sandy."

"And then?"

There was a startled exclamation behind them, and Shorty leaped out of the shrubbery, where he had been hiding all this while, to guard his master from any dangerous effects from the conversation with this strange child of nature.

"Look sharp!" gasped out Shorty. "There's a grizzly as big as a barn right at my heels!"

# 12

Swinging his own rifle under the pit of his arm, Peter Dunstan said: "Throw a stone, and the big brute'll scamper away fast enough."

"He ain't that kind of a bear," objected Shorty. "He come for me like he knew all about men folks and wanted to examine me for what kept me running. Y'understand? He came up like he meant business, and there — there he is now!"

He pitched the butt of his rifle into the hollow of his shoulder at the same moment that a great black grizzly — or one so dark-coated that it actually seemed black in this dim firelight, reared from among the bushes and stood before them. An eight or nine hundred pound monster such as had never before come into even the dreams of big Peter Dunstan or Shorty — old hunters though they were.

The giant greeted them with its vast paws folded on its stomach and a growl that seemed to fill the forest and far corners of the night.

In another instant, there would have been launched at its vitals two streams of lead from the highpower repeating rifles of the men had not the voice of Sandy Sweyn broken in with a harsh shout.

It carried a note in it such as Dunstan had never heard before in the voice of any man. It seemed to shrivel up its strength. It made the hand which steadied his rifle shake like a dead leaf in the wind. There was an evident prohibition in the command that made the trigger finger turn numb and refuse to contract. He did not have to look at Shorty to know that his cowpuncher felt the same sensations.

Then, to Dunstan's utter confusion of soul and mind, Sandy Sweyn leaped between them and the bear — leaped in between with his arms outstretched.

"Don't shoot!" said Sandy Sweyn. "He'll do you no harm. Don't shoot, partners!"

He backed up as he spoke, until he came fairly within reach of the monster. Aye, and the two arms, each as thick as a beam, unfolded, extended, and seemed about to take Sandy in a bone-crushing hug.

No, only one of them touched lightly on the shoulder of the man and stayed there.

Shorty, who recovered his wits first, after sight of this, whispered, "He's tamed a plumb wild grizzly."

"He'll do you not a mite of harm," said

141

Sandy calmly. "He was just wandering around and seeing who my visitors might be. There's no trouble in him!"

With the flat of his hand, he smote the great, muscle-cushioned shoulder of the black giant.

Peter Dunstan cast an anxious glance over his shoulder.

"Have you got any more pets hanging around, Sandy?" he asked. "Because my life insurance has run out, and I don't want to get into your family circle without being pretty well covered."

"There's no more to speak of," said Sandy, as the black bear pitched to his feet and then sat down, with the hand of his master resting on his shoulder. "But there's one mean one, that don't get on with me very well. He's sort of offish."

He raised his two thumbs to his mouth and whistled a screeching note through them. For answer, there immediately came a harsh spitting close at hand.

"There he is!" murmured Sandy Sweyn, and smiled, while a faint, malicious light gleamed for an instant in his eyes. "He's generally close by, but he don't like to show himself none. He hates to have your eye on him, you know!"

He called: "Come here, boy."

Among the shadows, Peter Dunstan saw two

round, gleaming eyes. Then a bobcat crawled forth on his belly, lashing his flanks with his long tail. On the verge of the firelight he crouched, blinking.

"I ain't gunna torture him by bringing him closer," said Sandy Sweyn. "He hates me and everybody else, except himself. He's a queer one. Run along, boy."

He waved his hand, and the big cat was gone, while Dunstan and Shorty exchanged mute glances.

"But Jim, here," went on the man of the woods, "he's my regular family. I'm wondering, sort of, how he would get along with the dog. What might the dog's name be?"

"His name is Chris," answered Dunstan.

Sandy, with some difficulty, freed the chain from the place where it was fastened about the tree. Then he carried the dog in his arms and placed him between the forepaws of the great bear.

Jim curled back his paws from the cowering sheep dog and lowered his great head to sniff at the puppy. His lip curled. One champ of those jaws would break every bone in the dog's body. Still Jim forebore. While the other two men stood by in wonder, they saw Chris, under the ministering hands of Sandy, lift his own head a little and begin to thump the ground with his tail in a most conciliatory fashion. Big Jim finally heaved his bulk up and, with his head turned to the side, and his small pig-eyes glittering, left the clearing with a rumbling growl.

"Jealous!" interpreted Sandy Sweyn. "He's jealous, d'ye see? Even jealous of the cat. I never seen such a bear! Eight hundred pounds of foolishness, pretty near."

He laughed and patted the head of Chris, who straightened and began to whine with pleasure, now that the grizzly was gone from sight.

"He's a brave dog," said Sandy. "You could see that, eh? Put his head right up, even with Jim leaning over him. I'll tell you, I'll have a time, though, getting Jim used to the pup. Might I have the dog *before* I get the mare, Mr. Dunstan? To give him back, y'understand, if I don't catch her for you!"

Peter Dunstan shook his head.

"Business is business, Sandy," said he. "You get the horse for me and deliver that horse to me right at the door of my ranch house. Then you'll get Chris, safe and sound. But if the horse died while you were hunting for her, or if somebody else got her first — why, Sandy, you have to admit that these things happen — you might be so attached to Chris, by that time, that you'd hate to give him up."

To this logic of the business man, Sandy Sweyn listened with his head bent to one side.

"I suppose that you're right," said he, at the last. "I don't seem to have any way of answering what you've just said. But I'll have that mare down at your place inside of a couple of weeks, or else I'll bust."

"Will you shake hands on that, Sandy?"

"Sure."

Their hands closed upon one another.

Sandy Sweyn stepped back. He looked up — and a broad moon with a yellow-figured face was drifting up among the trees.

"Why," said Sandy uneasily, "I suppose that there ain't any time better than right now, for starting. So long!"

He turned instantly from the clearing.

As for the men that he left behind him, they sat down and stared rather helplessly at one another.

"You look sort of wild, Shorty."

"I was just thinking of something."

"And what's that?"

"How empty-looking his eyes are, mostly."

"Aye."

"But when he jumped in front of us — you remember? — his eyes were blazin' like the eyes of that cat, when it sneaked up to the edge of the fire. And I thought — I couldn't help thinkin' —" Shorty paused.

145

"Well?" asked Peter Dunstan.

"I guess it was the same thought that *you* had, chief, for that matter. And I'll name it, too. I figured that if I was to turn loose some of the bullets right into his hide, while he stood there in front of us, that maybe I would be doing the world a good turn!"

Peter Dunstan nodded solemnly. "I had the same idea," he admitted. "Because it occurred to me that if he should ever start and run amuck among other folks, he would smash up a dozen or two good men before he more than got warmed up. Some day, he'll make a killing that will make the worst things that Wild Bill ever did, look like fifty cents."

Shorty paused in his task of stamping out the fire, to look up and nod. They said no more, but presently they went to their horses, mounted, and started out across the forest. If they had luck, they could get back to the village by midnight.

They threaded their way until they came to a more or less obliterated trail that wound along in the general direction which they wished to follow.

"What put the idea into your head — of baiting him with a yelling dog?" asked Peter Dunstan.

"I dunno. I remembered him and the gelding at the ranch — and then the queer look in his eyes, as if he understood things that can't talk."

"Shorty, you got a great head. Isn't that a galloping horse that we hear?"

Suddenly, across the face of the hill that rolled out naked from the shadows of the forest, they saw a rider on a speeding horse — a great-striding animal that showed only for an instant, and then was gone.

"There he goes!" whispered Peter Dunstan. "More luck to him. Darn his queer heart!"

"Mind the dog!" called Shorty.

Chris was struggling forward with all his might, straining against the lariat by which he was being led along, vainly endeavoring to follow the fleeing rider through the night.

# 13

Of all the moments in that Iliad of horse adventure, none matched with one that happened in the fag-end of a long, hot day on the Condon Desert. For the two foremost pursuers of the mare combined their efforts to capture her.

It would have been difficult to select two men of types more opposite. José Rezan you have already seen, big, blond, splendid in his beauty and in his strength. John Lucas came from somewhere in the Vermont mountains. He was made long and narrow, body and head. His thin face seemed to have been designed to cleave through the wind with the least resistance. His neck was like the crooked neck of a bird.

There was nothing about him of a manly size except his arms and his legs. They were long and strong, and John Lucas added to their animal strength an animal quickness. He was like a big snake, just as José Rezan was like a big lion, tawny and grand.

These two came together. Each had appeared as a hero more than once in the epic hunt for the white mare. José Rezan suggested that they join forces to see if they might not compass her capture.

"But," said John Lucas, "suppose that we get her. Who'll be the lucky man?"

"You take the money," said José Rezan, "and I'll take the girl."

John Lucas thrust forward his long, lean chin.

"I'll have the money *and* the girl," said he ominously.

"Very well," answered José Rezan, without bitterness and without fear. "We'll wait till we have Elena Blanca. After she's ours, then we'll fight for her, you and I — a good fair fight, eh?"

John Lucas thrust out his brown hand.

"We'll make that a bargain!" said he.

They gathered their best horses, employed the cleverest helpers that they could find, and laid their plans with such effect that during half a day they harried the beautiful white mare, driving her not fast enough to come up with her, but continually turning her toward points where fresh horses would be available to take up the labor.

Twice, as she streamed through the heat of the afternoon with the sun burning on her silver body, it seemed to José Rezan that she must be theirs — and twice she found in her

149

strong, wild heart an extra fund of energy, and drew away from the pursuit.

It was not until the golden time of the day, when the sun was low in the western sky, that magical moment on the desert when the period of rosy light has not yet quite begun and the white light of the stronger sun has ended, that Elena Blanca broke suddenly across the line of the pursuit. She struck off for the mouth of a ravine that pointed into the broader valley, with all one side of it painted with gold and all the other side clouded in purple.

In vain John Lucas and big José Rezan offered their best riding and strove with quirt and spur to get a little more power into the legs of their horses. They simply had not the speed. To be sure, they had not run, either of them, a tithe of the distance that the white mare had covered on this day. On the other hand, she was not carrying the weight of a heavy man, nor the gripping burden of a ponderous range saddle, equipped with two biting cinches that hugged belly and chest. Neither was she worried by spur and whip. She flew across the desert, urged by the vision before her of liberty, and hounded by the dread of slavery behind.

She left them behind her with every stride. She was tired but still had an untapped store of nerve, energy and pride to call upon. It seemed to the despairing pursuers that she ran as freely and as freshly as she had that morning when the first sight of them sent her drifting away downwind.

She darted into the mouth of the ravine. Perhaps it was a blind alley into which she had dipped? They flogged their frantic horses, but there was no more speed in them. They could rock along all day and not mind the labor of the canter greatly, but to gallop a single mile behind Elena Blanca was a killing thing. They were spent; their heads were up; their hoofs beat hard upon the ground. The spring was out of their stride.

When they reached the mouth of the ravine, the two saw White Helen running lightly far before, and making for the uplands. At that moment, as they were about to resign themselves to the inevitable and draw rein, out of the shadows of the western side of the valley there started a rider on a strong blue roan — a long-striding creature that plunged after Elena Blanca.

She met that challenge with a stout heart. She tossed her little head, and with pricking ears drew upon her great soul for greater and greater speed. The speed was there to be drawn forth. She darted with wonderful beauty of gait straight up the valley, like a true blood horse when it answers the call of its jockey and fights down the home stretch.

That frantic galloping did not settle the issue in this instance. The rider on the blue horse was not distanced. He was not even put slightly to the rear. At once the two wondering observers could see that the reaching stride of the blue roan was gradually swinging up on Elena Blanca at every stride.

Aye, she had done great running and long running on this day. Even when she was fresh and free, could she have withstood this challenge?

She had still more to call upon. She flattened her ears in her desperation. She pushed forward with a desperate earnestness. It was not enough, and the blue horse gained still more rapidly.

Then a rounding elbow of the valley wall came between the two leaders and the two behind. When the latter were in view again, they found that the blue horse ran literally almost side by side with the little white mare. She, with tossing, frantic head, strove to get more way; strove to shake off this cruel runner, and strove in vain!

John Lucas drew rein suddenly, crying, "He's only playing with Elena! He's only playing with her, old son. We could ride all night, but we'd never see him capture her. He'll take the heart out of her first, and then he'll take her when she has no more spirit in her than a lamb!"

The white mare and the great blue roan disappeared into the highlands, while the two pursuers remained in the lowlands, staring with a deep wonder in the direction in which they had disappeared.

"He could never have come up to her like that," vowed José Rezan, "if she had had her strength at the end of the day."

"I dunno," said Lucas. "She's tired, and she's run a good many tens of miles to-day. But still, I don't know. I wouldn't want to bet on how fast that blue hoss could run, even with a heavy man like that in the saddle. It's got a stride made of rubber, that blue hoss has. I never seen anything like the way it walked right up on Elena Blanca. I never seen nothing like it. I wouldn't of believed that even a thoroughbred race hoss could of closed up on her like that. But it ain't just the running of the blue hoss that has me wondering!"

"What is it, then?" asked José.

"What I wonder at, is how did the gent that's riding that hoss know that Elena would be taking her run up this here canyon? How did he come to be waiting here so pat?"

José Rezan nodded.

"Maybe," said he, "the rest of these canyons

are all blind — no easy way through them to the mountains behind. And so he waited here, thinking that *she* would know. Because that little white devil of a mare, she knows a great deal more than we think!"

"You can explain it," muttered John Lucas, "but I say that it's strange, and ain't likely. It's as though he could of read the mind of that hoss, friend. And that's what I sort of believe!"

In the meantime, Elena Blanca had reached the high broken lands toward which the ravine pointed. There, with coverts on every side, she felt a greater security. There was still no escape, for the rider on the blue roan mare kept close at her side. When she wheeled, the blue horse wheeled likewise. When she dodged, she could not put any distance between herself and the pursuer.

Despair began to steal the strength of the white mare, more than had all her heroic running of this famous day. The golden time of the afternoon ended, and the clouds in the west were masses of red flame when Elena Blanca, at last, came to a halt and stood upon wide-braced legs, her head hanging low, the fire gone from her eyes.

She waited patiently for the rush of the victor, the shout of triumph, and the sting and burn of the deadly rope around her neck. There was no charge, no shout, no hiss of the rope above her head. Instead, she saw the man dismount and come toward her with gentle words, his hand outstretched. The great blue roan was following him, willingly, with pricked ears.

Elena Blanca tossed her head and started off at a rickety gallop. Presently the blue mare and her rider were at her heels again. Elena turned and paused, and whinnied faintly, more in wonder than in terror and despair. Once more the stranger came toward her with a gentle voice and an extended hand.

# 14

The news traveled on wings, as a miracle accomplished. After all their labors, all their weeks and weeks of patient striving, here came a man who, in a single day, did what all their work had not been able to accomplish.

The news traveled far to the south. On an instant wing, it reached the town nearest to the ranch of big Peter Dunstan and sent a messenger carrying the rumor forth along the road toward the rancher's house.

Peter Dunstan was heavily occupied on that morning. One of his oldest and best cowpunchers, Macfarlane, had just come in with a ringing complaint.

"How long might I of been working for you, Dunstan?"

"Nine years, Mack!"

"Am I reasonable or unreasonable?"

"Except when you've been hitting up the redeye — mighty reasonable, Mack."

"What have I got that's better than anything else?"

"Why, your old cutting horse, Sam, I suppose."

"Would you mind coming out and having a look at Sam, now?"

Peter Dunstan stepped to the door, and yonder was Sam, an ugly-headed bay horse, hobbling from one bunch of dead grass to the next, with a great limp in his off foreleg.

"What the devil has done that, Mack?"

"Look yonder!"

With a savage face, Mack indicated a little heap of black and white curled up in the shadow of one of the big posts of the nearest corral.

"It's that new dog that you brung down from the north with you, Dunstan. It's that Chris. He's been seen houndin' old Sam around the corral, and finally, he run that hoss agin' a post — and there you see!"

"I'm sorry, Mack. I'm terribly sorry!"

"Sorry is one thing. But a sorry *dog* is what I want to see. A dead dog out yonder would be a heap of use to me, Dunstan."

"You want me to kill Chris?"

"What *use* might he be here?" asked Macfarlane savagely. "Or maybe you're gunna start drifting sheep on this here ranch?"

At this sarcastic proposal, even big Peter Dunstan winced.

"I'll never run sheep on this place. You know that. But I'll tell you what I'll do, Mack. I'll tie up that dog till it gets a little sense.

Only — I can't shoot it. I've got a use for it."

Macfarlane removed his hat and scratched his half-bald head.

"If he runs that hoss of mine ag'in," said he, "I blow for another bunkhouse, and I take my Sam along with me. Dogs is all right, in their place. But their place ain't never been in the running of hoss flesh, and it ain't never gunna be. So long, chief!"

Macfarlane retreated toward Sam and led the cutting horse back to the corral, while the rancher took young Chris by the collar and tied him with a strong length of new rope to a sapling beside the house.

He went back to his office to wade through a stack of bills with his checkbook beside him — a dreary task. His payments were always slow for the mere reason that he detested these clerical duties with all his soul. He had not removed more than the top of the pile when a sharp, mischievous barking sounded from the corrals. Rising to look out the window, he saw Chris, with a chewed-off rope end flying from his neck, in hot pursuit of Sam.

Poor Sam, crippled and staggering, dodged and kicked as well as he could. But the wisdom of old inherited craft was working in the brain of Chris, and he rounded Sam neatly into a corner, where the gelding made a frantic and vain endeavor to jump the fence. He merely crashed against the top bar and sprawled back again into the dust of the corral.

"Chris!" yelled Peter Dunstan. "Hey, Chris!"

Chris was far too delighted with his work to listen to any human voice. He circled Sam with a wild outburst of yapping.

"Chris! Will you hear me? Chris! I'll kill you, you fool — Chris!"

The gun came into the hand of Peter Dunstan. It was not a carefully aimed shot. It was rather a random try, directed by chance. But poor Chris leaped high into the air and came down with a death screech, flat upon his side, and lay still.

Peter Dunstan did not wait to go through the doorway. He swung himself through the big window and reached the spot in an instant. He knew even before he started that it was useless to make an examination. Something in the mere yell of the dog had been enough to tell him that its life went out with the last of its cry. When he reached Chris, the lolling tongue in the dust and the glazed eyes were an unnecessary proof.

Macfarlane, at that instant, came on a galloping horse around the corner of the barn.

"Did I hear that dog yelpin' again at the

heels of my Sam?" he shouted.

"The devil with you, and your horse. Take this dog, and bury him — and bury him deep — and don't let me hear another word out of you for a month!"

Big Dunstan turned upon his heel, and Macfarlane was too astonished and overawed to protest against the shameful burden which was thus thrust upon his shoulders. He knew his own value, and he knew that this employer knew it, also. It was as though the heavens had fallen upon Macfarlane's head.

Peter Dunstan, as he strode gloomily back toward the house, saw a small dust cloud rising far down the road.

"It's the news," said he to his gloomily prophetic heart, "that the kid has taken Elena Blanca and is bringin' her south to me. And me with the kid's payment lying yonder dead as a doornail! Oh, to blazes with Macfarlane and his horse — and ropes that a fool dog can chew through!"

So said the rancher to himself, even before the figure of the messenger could be described through the dust cloud. For once, his prophecy was true.

Two things stood in Peter Dunstan's way. One was that it was known that the dog was dead. The other was that he was on his ranch where all men knew more or less about Sandy and Sandy's prowess. If he tried to gather among them two or three willing to confront Sandy in wrath, it would be a hard task to find them.

He made his decision on the spot.

First of all, he went to find Macfarlane. He found him heaping up and trampling down the mound over the spot where he had buried poor little Chris. As Peter Dunstan looked on, something like remorse stirred in him, and a vague feeling of dread, lest the evil impulse which had destroyed the dog should bring unhappy consequences upon him in the future.

On the whole, Dunstan was as little given to remorse or to the pangs of conscience as any man in the world. He trampled on this tender gloom as Macfarlane was even then trampling upon the grave of the dead puppy.

"Mack," said the rancher, "there's nobody in the world that knows about the death of that pup except you and me. You understand?"

"Why, that's straight enough," answered the cowpuncher.

"And, just now, I don't *want* any others to know. You hear?"

"You don't want anybody else to know," said Macfarlane, scenting a mystery with quivering nostrils. "Well, I'll keep it dark enough, then."

"Here's the main point. I'm riding out and taking that dog along with me."

"You're riding out," repeated Macfarlane, to get his lesson firmly in mind, "and you're going to take the dog along with you. I get that. What's next?"

"There's nothing next, so far as any of the boys on the ranch are concerned. But somewhere inside of the next two or three days, Sandy Sweyn is going to come back here, riding his blue roan."

"Sandy back!" exclaimed Macfarlane, and his eyes opened a little.

"You don't like Sandy?" asked the rancher curiously.

"I don't like nothing that I ain't able to understand," said the sullen puncher. "Why?"

"You're like me," agreed Dunstan. "You don't like anything that's too ghostly. I'm with you on that. But now, old son, the point of this yarn is that Sandy Sweyn is going to have something else with him — and that something is going to be Elena Blanca, that all the fuss has been made about."

Macfarlane took off his hat and gaped at his employer.

"The white mare!" said he. "And then — the girl —"

Peter Dunstan held the eye of the other with a glance like a bar of iron.

"The girl is out of it!" said Dunstan. "That boy is a half-wit, as you know."

"He's a half-wit, or worse. He's plain batty, by my way of thinking. But — are you dead sure?"

"I'm sure that he's got Elena Blanca. There's no doubt about that. He's coming down here to find me and turn that mare over to me."

"You lucky devil!" muttered the cowpuncher. "*You're* the one that gets —"

"And what he is going to ask for after he gives it to me, is the puppy. Do you get this?"

"Every word!" exclaimed Macfarlane. "That's why that dog was so important, eh? He was the pay that that fool, Sweyn, got for bringing down that —"

"You can do all the thinking that you want to, Mack," said Dunstan. "I can't keep you from it, and you're too smart not to think things out pretty straight. But do your thinking to yourself. I've got no time to explain things to you, or I would. The fact is that when he comes down here and asks about the dog, you are to tell him that I've gone off with Chris. Is that clear?"

"Yes. I've got that, right enough."

"Then if he says that he's brought the mare for me and wants to know where to find me — and the dog — you're to try to get him to leave the mare here with you. If he'll do it, you're to put a pair of robes on her and put her in that high-fenced corral, and then mount one of the boys guard over her, night and day."

"Right! Because she means something to you!"

"She does, of course! But perhaps Sandy won't want to turn her over to any one other than myself. If you can't persuade him to part with Elena, then you'll have to tell him that I've gone — to Chorleywood!"

"Chorleywood!" gasped out Macfarlane. "Chorleywood?"

"That's what I said, man. Chorleywood!"

"Chief," said the other gravely, "you ain't forgot that the boys over that way don't look on you as being any uncle of theirs!"

"I've not forgotten them any more than they've forgotten me," declared big Peter Dunstan. "But the thing for you to remember, Macfarlane, is just this — that I've gone to Chorleywood, and that I've taken the dog, Chris, along with me. When you remember that, you can stop working your brain. And to the boys here on the ranch, you don't know even that much. You only know that I've ridden off, and that I've taken the dog with me. One thing more, Mack, if this thing goes through smoothly, you're not going to lose anything by it. Here's a twenty to stick in your hip pocket. And there'll be a good deal more than that when the deal is all finished. So long, Mack!"

Not waiting for any reply, he turned on his heel and strode away, with Macfarlane staring helplessly after him.

That one word had frozen his brain and made him incapable of thinking. All that he could see, at that moment, was a time five years before, when the rustlers and crooks at Chorleywood had dared to lay hand upon some of the cattle of the "chief." The result had been a stern campaign. Peter Dunstan gathered all his cowhands. He brought in recruits at the handsome tune of ten dollars a day, and keep. With a little army of fifty, all told, he started for the outlaws without asking leave of the State.

He did not need to ask leave. Three governors had admitted that Chorleywood was a sore spot on the political map. Yet three governors had been unable to deal with the menace, from which a score, or more, of criminals had been in the habit of issuing forth at their pleasure and executing their schemes before they returned to their well-known "hole-in-the-wall" country.

The fifty hard riders of Peter Dunstan had labored during a whole month. It was their boast that they made Chorleywood too hot to hold the crooks. They lost two good fighters, and half a dozen were more or less badly wounded, and an uncounted number injured, carrying back with their column no fewer than four men upon each of whose heads there was a handsome reward placed by the State or by the Federal government. It was said that the government had had to pay for Peter Dunstan's little hunting party, and had given him all his fun and a little surplus of cash besides!

Not only had he effectually broken up the gang for the moment, but he had well-nigh ruined their morale. For a long time hard-pressed criminals in distant parts of the country forgot to look toward Chorleywood as a haven of refuge.

However, five years on the borderline of the law is a long time. Before it had half lapsed, the old gathering of yeggs and bad ones of one sort or another commenced to reassemble. As they gathered, they made one eternal rule, that no matter where they trespassed, it must not be upon the lands of Peter Dunstan.

Having been burned once, they rightly feared the fire, but following the same rule, was not Peter Dunstan a madman to venture his head in such society?

# 15

As a matter of fact, Peter Dunstan had not made up his mind on the spur of the moment. It was only after the most mature consideration that he had decided that he would have to go to Chorleywood. The impulse which drove him was, not excepting even his love of money and power, the greatest that had ever entered his life. It was the love of little Catalina Mirandos.

When he came in sight of the mountains of Chorleywood, like a mighty green ocean, with all the waves torn to jagged edges by the pressure of a gale, he paused in doubt. Yonder, he knew, were men who would ask for nothing better than to put a pistol to his head. At last, he drew from his pocket the newspaper clipping which contained the picture of pretty Señorita Mirandos. One sight of her face was enough to remove all his doubts.

He dismounted and looked to his horse. The way had been long and dusty, but the gelding had stood the labor well. Its head was still high, and its eye bright. If Dunstan had to ride for his life, the horse could give a good account of itself, beyond any reasonable doubt.

He had not been here in five years. Then he had ridden with fifty fighting men at his back. There was a reason, therefore, in the care with which he proceeded. When he rounded a forest-clad shoulder of a steep mountainside and saw a little shack before him, he reined his horse sharply back into the shadows of the pines again.

However, he had not come to avoid men, but to find them. This was as good a spot as any in which to begin. He sent the gelding forth again. When he leaned from the saddle, and tapped the wall with the handle of his quirt — holding the whip in his left hand, as a natural precaution which left his gun hand free — no one answered.

He was relieved, for a moment. When he dismounted and stepped through the door, he saw that a fire burned in the stove and a kettle steamed upon it. There had been men in that room hardly a minute before. The air was still thick with the smoke from their pipes. Yonder was half a side of bacon, in the act of being turned into thick, white, gleaming slices.

His coming had frightened the inhabitants away. Certainly here was enough proof that he was in the center of Chorleywood, where every stranger was a danger to every other man! There was only one vital consolation — the men did not know him. Otherwise, they might have begun with rifle bullets on him. As it was, they were lying low, somewhere, watching him from the edge of the trees, striving to make out what manner of man he might be.

He set their doubts at rest in the most eloquent fashion known to a Westerner. He issued from the cabin once more, unsaddled and unbridled his horse, hobbled him, and turned him loose to graze. Then, carrying saddle and bridle, he reentered the house and stood in the doorway, holding the bridle over his left arm.

The response to this summons, delivered as it was by silent gestures only, was in keeping with the character of Chorleywood. Suddenly, Mr. Dunstan was aware of a shadow standing nearby, at the corner of the house.

Yet he did not turn his head. He steeled himself with a great effort, though he was aware that another shadow had come up on the far side of the shack and stood at the opposite corner of the house.

"Well?" asked the man on his right suddenly.

Peter Dunstan allowed his head to turn slowly toward the speaker. He saw a low, broad-built fellow with a fat body and great shovel-shaped feet. His face was strangely pale and intellectual — in contrast to his body and the clothes in which that body was equipped.

"Well," said Dunstan, "how's things?"

"Slow," said the fat man, "but pretty easy. How's things with you, stranger?"

"Fast," said Peter Dunstan, "and not so easy."

A sudden smile flashed upon the face of the other. A smile of infinite understanding. He felt that he was recognizing a real blood brother in crime.

"What's your name?" asked he.

"Pete," said Dunstan.

"Aye, but what Pete? 'Denver Pete?' 'Cheyenne Pete?' 'Chi Pete,' or what?"

"To-morrow," said Dunstan, "maybe I'll be one kind or other of Pete, but to-night I'm just that."

The other nodded. "I'm Lawrie," said he. "And this is Mike."

Dunstan turned about and faced a villainous-looking rascal with a week's red beard like thick rust upon his face. Mike blinked his eyes at the stranger and nodded; there was no word said between them. Turning into the house, Dunstan put the seal upon his claim for hospitality by hanging his saddle by a stirrup from a peg on the wall, and his bridle over the horn.

After that, he lent his hand to the cooking. They were hungry, all three, and until they had finished frying bacon, and eating it between cold, thick slices of pone, washed down with coffee, black as night and strong as lye, there was no further talk. When the meal was ended, and the claim of Dunstan upon the hospitality and friendship of the others thus established, Lawrie leaned across the rickety table and said:

"Now, Pete, you've got us where you want us. We can't pull a knife or a gun on you when your back is turned, not unless we want the same thing to happen to us, the next time that we run for cover. So what's your name?"

Mike stared at Dunstan out of bleared eyes.

"My name," said the guest, "is Peter Dunstan."

He sat back to watch the effect of the hurling of this bomb.

It made Mike stiffen in his place, with rapidly blinking eyes; but Lawrie sprang to his feet, with a gun leaping from cover faster than thought.

"*You're* Dunstan?" he exclaimed. "*You're* Dunstan?"

Then, remembering how fast the laws of hospitality bound him, he thrust the revolver back into its holster.

"And I might have drilled you clean while

171

you stood in the door of the shack! I *wanted* to drill you, because I thought that there was a look about you that meant trouble! And now here you are — and *safe* from me!"

Even the steady nerves of Dunstan were troubled by this violent outburst.

"I've never met you before, Lawrie," said he. "How have I ever managed to step on your toes?"

"Five years ago I had a pal here in Chorleywood," said Lawrie, eying the other with a fixed malevolence. "And you and your gang did for him — as *you'll* be done for, before ever you see your way clear of the trees again!"

"Will they be hot to get at me?" asked Dunstan.

The other grinned with concentrated satisfaction.

"I don't need to use my own hands on you, or my own guns," said he. "I can keep clean out of it — except just to spread the word that you're here. Only — I'd like to know what sort of a fool you are to put your head right into the fire, like this!"

"Would you?" said Dunstan steadily. "Then, I'll tell you. I put my head into the fire, partner —"

"You're no partner of mine!"

"I came here to Chorleywood because I need help."

"And the boys here having been old chums of yours — and you having done such a lot for us — you know that you can get what you need out of us?" asked Lawrie sarcastically.

"I know," said Peter Dunstan, "that I kept my hands off you until you began to bother my cows. And then I raised the devil for you! But after that, we've let each other alone. I know another thing: By doing me a good turn now, you boys can make a neat little haul in hard cash. You understand? When I need help, I'm willing to pay for it!"

Lawrie nodded. He was fairly white with scorn and with rage.

"Money'll buy anything," said he, "starting right in with man. So you're going to buy us?"

"I'll buy you afterward," said Peter Dunstan. "But I'll fight you first. When you spread the news around that I'm here, tell the boys that if any of them have a grudge against me that won't stand wear, I'm here to meet him fair and square. I've got a gun, and the other fellow will have a gun. We'll fight it out here in the clearing in front of your shack, until I finish them, one by one, or until one of them drops me. And that goes for you, Lawrie, along with the rest.

"If you ache for a fight to clear your conscience, I'm the last man in the world to make things hard and slow for you. There's lots of room outside, and we have our guns at our hips. Step out with me, Lawrie, if you want a square deal. If you down me, that's the end. If I down you, my friend Mike, here, will take the word through Chorleywood that I'm here, and that I'm ready to pay."

He hesitated a long moment, seeing the hate flicker out of the cunning eyes of Lawrie, and cunning brighten them instead.

"You've had chuck in my house," said Lawrie, "and you ought to know that you're safe from me. But the other boys — there'll be some of them that'll take it in another way, your being here. I'm starting now, old-timer. And maybe you'll have new callers before sunset!"

A man without fear is usually a man without sense, but no one could accuse the rancher of being a fool. It was a long and anxious time that he spent in the shack, in the company of Mike. He spent that time in talk — the talk of Mike, not his own. Finding himself with a celebrity, Mike was glad of an opportunity to unbosom himself of his thoughts and his deeds.

But he stopped the easy flow of his narrative at a sign from big Peter Dunstan. He had risen from the chunk of log which he was using as a stool. As he rose, he turned toward the door and brought out a Colt. His hat, caught over the muzzle of his Colt, he extended cautiously past the door jamb — held it there for a moment — and then hastily withdrew it.

Mike, understanding, sneaked into a far corner of the shack and crouched there, grinning and shaking with expectancy like a drunkard eying a glass of whisky which he has not the price to buy.

Big Peter Dunstan, as he pushed the hat out a second time, received what he wanted — the bark of a revolver from the farther side of the clearing, and a sharp twitch which knocked the hat spinning from the Colt.

His eye was at the door in an instant. Yonder he saw a tall form rising from a screening bush with a yell of triumph. It was a long shot for even the best of Colts, but Peter Dunstan risked it, with a quick snapshot. He saw the man in the brush run forward a blundering step or two, then fall heavily upon his face — down, but not dead. He lay yonder, twitching and then writhing convulsively.

"Lemme get to him!" said Mike, in a passion of commiseration. "*I've* been down just like that!"

When he reached the door, he struck the

arm of Peter Dunstan, like a bar of iron, beating him back.

"He's got pals behind him," said Dunstan, "and we want to know just who they are."

Certainly the groaning of the wounded man in the clearing might have moved any torturer, but Dunstan was serene. Presently a voice shouted:

"Dunstan, give us a chance to help him, and we'll give you a chance to get away."

Other voices broke in, in agreement.

"Who are you?" shouted Dunstan in answer.

"I'm Coudray."

That name was vaguely familiar to the ear of Dunstan. It was connected, by rumor, with sundry atrocities on the highway. It was not the most famous name in the Chorleywood.

Dunstan answered in a ringing voice: "I'll talk to Simonides, and nobody else. If Simonides is not there, I'll take my chances with the rest of you, but if he's there, I'll dicker with him."

Simonides, the little Greek, had written himself large in the recent history of Chorleywood. Of all the criminals who had sought shelter there, he was far the most famous; of all who had dwelt there among the mountains and the evergreens, none had behind him so long a list of dead men, of wrecked bank safes, of prodigies of cunning and invention.

He had risen to fame first as a great counterfeiter. He had gone on growing in importance after skillful detectives broke up his gang for manufacturing and pushing "the queer." Now it was said that no man led a successful life of crime in the West except by the direction or the connivance of Simonides.

Now a voice answered from the edge of the woods — a voice pitched just high enough to carry to Peter Dunstan without effort:

"Here I am, Dunstan. I'm Simonides. If you want my word for your safety, you'll have it."

"Simonides, I hear you. And I take you at your word. You boys are free to take up the chap I winged. Hop to it!"

"All right, men!" called the calm, strong voice of Simonides. "Get to him!"

The numbers that responded sent a shiver down the back of Dunstan. For he knew that he had long been hated in Chorleywood, but he did not dream, really, that the power of his name could draw so many enemies about him, and so quickly. Now a full half dozen men hurried out from the covert of the trees toward their fallen comrade.

There were others as well, to say nothing of Simonides himself, who now stepped from the trees — a little man with a great, Napoleonic head. He wore an air of distinction; he stepped as one in authority. Peter Dunstan saw that he had made a ten-strike when he placed himself, more or less, in the hands of this formidable outlaw.

He came straight up to Dunstan and shook hands with him, saying, "I thought that I'd be looking at your dead face, Dunstan, when we all started for the shack, here. But perhaps we can patch things up pretty well. Tell me what's brought you here?"

Honesty, as Dunstan could very well see, was the usual policy of this arch-criminal. His dissimulation he reserved for great events of death or of plunder. In his usual intercourse with other men, no matter what crude criminals they might be, he chose to be bluntly frank, hyper-honest.

"First," said Dunstan, "tell me who I dropped. He must be some important man."

"Why?"

"By the willingness of you all to make a bargain to save his hide."

"That means nothing at all," answered Simonides, turning his great, black, considerate eyes up to the face of the tall rancher. "When we're here in Chorleywood, we pretend to be very fond of each other. But after all, there is *some* sense in this mutual devotion in Chorleywood. You save me when I'm in danger; then you can depend upon it that I shall try to save you.

"I have known yeggs who rode five hundred miles from Chorleywood to go to the help of a man they had never heard of before, simply because they knew that he was a fellow crook. You understand how it is — the romantic idea, something for nothing, the forlorn hope, the necessity that all of us have in believing in our virtues as individuals and even as a class — that's what creates the bonds between us rascals here in Chorleywood. Down in our more honest hearts, that so seldom influence our actions, we know that we are great liars and hypocrites."

It was in many ways the most astonishing speech that Peter Dunstan had ever heard. He watched the speaker from the corner of his eyes. On the other hand he watched the crooks of Chorleywood tenderly caring for the wounded man, binding up his hurt, and then carrying him away in an improvised stretcher.

"Through the hip," said Mr. Simonides, nodding. "Very painful, that. I think I had rather be shot through the body, though that is painful enough!"

He spoke with quiet authority, and well he might, for legend declared that Simonides had been blown almost to bits, one time or another in his exciting career by the bullets of the men of the law, or of rivals in his own profession.

"Now, Dunstan, what has brought you here?"

"Necessity," said Dunstan.

"Bah!" exclaimed the other. "Do you imagine that I thought you had come here for fun? Who do you want robbed or murdered, Dunstan?"

The latter started.

"Robbed or murdered?" he echoed. "I don't want either." He checked himself abruptly: "That is to say —"

"Good!" said the outlaw. "You may as well be perfectly honest from the start! What is it, man?"

"In the first place," said Dunstan, "I don't know how serious this affair may be. You understand me?"

"Very well. I'll use my imagination."

"In the second place, I want to find out how I can be useful to you before I ask you to be useful to me."

"Friend," said Simonides, "you are supposed to be our great enemy. If we could use your ranch as a second Chorleywood, when in a pinch, it would be worth ten thousand a year — to me alone!"

"That is not enough," said the rancher.

The other whistled.

"You are going to put up a high price?"

"I am."

"What is it, Dunstan."

"Do I know you well enough to talk straight out?"

"You do," said Simonides. "I can be honest with you because I have not a thing to gain by lying to you. Go on and put your cards on the table."

"A poor half-wit youngster," said Dunstan, "is riding in this direction, I think, and bringing a horse toward my ranch. I won't go into all the details. I'll only tell you that with one man at my ranch I've left word that I'm at Chorleywood. The half-wit will start in this direction after me. Now, Simonides, I have to have the horse that he is bringing along with him."

"I knew that you were fond of good horse-flesh," said the outlaw, "but I didn't know that you were as fond as all of this. Go on, man. I'm interested."

"When the fellow comes here, I want that horse taken away from him and turned over to me."

"Look here," said Simonides solemnly, "do you mean to say that you respect the law so much that you wouldn't dare to take away from a half-wit anything that you wanted?"

"Simonides," said the other, "you're a keen

181

fellow. The law wouldn't hold me back. It's the fear of the half-wit that stops me."

"Fear of a half-wit!" cried Simonides.

"Exactly that. And, if you understand this job — to get the horse and turn it over to me — I want you to understand in the first place, Simonides, that you have taken on a man-sized job. I'm a fair hand with a gun. You're a much better one, perhaps. But if the two of us went out gunning for this simple-minded fellow, I'm afraid that the money would be on him, and not on us!"

# 16

While Dunstan and Simonides stood in comfortable conversation in the clearing at Chorleywood, a strange apparition appeared before the blinking eyes of the two toughest and oldest cowpunchers on the Dunstan ranch — namely, Shorty and Macfarlane.

They had barely finished dragging a stupid cow out of the muddy margin of a tank, where she had mired down almost to her back. Turning, almost too weary to curse, Shorty cried out in a loud voice and pointed up the slope. Mack, looking in the same direction, saw only a thick dust cloud blown down the shallow draw. As the sand mist dissipated, he was aware of the brilliant figure of a white horse — a dazzlingly bright form, as though cut out of a rock crystal. A moment later, he yelled to Shorty:

"It's Elena Blanca! It's White Helen!"

"Ride to the right!" cried Shorty in a voice made husky with terrible excitement and suspense. "I'll go to the left, and if we can cut in behind her and turn her down onto the ranch —"

For she was running freely down the draw, until she saw them and came to a stop — like a wild wolf, with a foot raised and her head high. As she was at that instant, with the sun burning upon her, and the wind combing out the silver of her mane and tail, there was never in the world a creature more beautiful!

Yet even then, the nearer approach to them did not seem to altogether daunt her. She turned her head and whinnied softly — then she actually advanced toward them again, down the draw!

The explanation was almost stranger than the fact. For now, above the farther side of the draw, there appeared Sandy Sweyn on the great blue roan. A dusty man on a dusty horse, like a poor attendant following a bright angel form — like a picture of labor following wearily after wild freedom.

"It's Sandy," said Macfarlane gloomily. "Just for a minute, I thought that you and me would have to shoot it out to see who had caught the mare! It's Sandy, and he ain't got her on a rope, even! Can you come over that?"

A call from Sandy, and the white mare whirled and darted back to his side. She looked no larger than a pony, as delicately lovely as any antelope, dancing along in the shadow of the great blue roan.

So Sandy Sweyn came down to the waiting pair. Sandy was not one to waste much time upon idle greetings. He merely wanted to know at once where he might find their master. Shorty answered:

"He rode off the other day taking a dog along with him —"

"Taking a dog along with him!" said Sandy sadly.

Macfarlane waved Shorty back: "I've got to talk to this gent alone," he cautioned his friend. He rode up close to the blue mare until his mustang touched noses with her.

"Sandy," he said, "the chief left word that you was to leave Elena Blanca here and ride over to meet him — and get the dog from him."

Sandy nodded, saying, "I'll take her to a corral." He paused abruptly. "But suppose that Mr. Dunstan won't believe that I've got her until he sees her — I'll have to ride clear back here with him — and I got to go north pretty quick. No, you tell me where to find him, and I'll take Elena Blanca along with me. Look at her, Mack. She's a pretty thing, ain't she?"

Macfarlane agreed with all his heart. Something kept him from trying to press the point and draw the mare from Sandy now and keep her at the ranch. He did not want to be inveigled into the war which was apt to follow between Dunstan and the half-wit.

"Go to Chorleywood, Sandy," he said. "You'll find that Dunstan is over there, some place. Ride to Chorleywood and look sharp around, and you'll find him —"

"The dog — Chris —" broke in Sandy, "how was he looking?"

"Pretty well," said Macfarlane tersely. "Pretty well, I suppose."

"It's a queer thing," said Sandy Sweyn, "how a dog will sneak along and step right into your heart, that way. Before you can hardly tell what's happening. I've been missin' that dog a pile ever since I last seen him. Which way lies Chorleywood from here?"

"Why, Sandy, you seen it every day while you was working here. There it is, north and east — that black smudge on the edge of the sky. D'you see?"

"I see it. I can make it by to-morrow morning."

"Easy. It ain't so far off as it looks."

"So long, Mack."

"So long, Sandy. But ain't you gunna stop in at the house and say 'hello' to the boys and have a cup of coffee, even, before you start along?"

"I'll start along the way that I'm fixed right now, Adios!"

He camped early that evening, before he had entered a mile into the green margin of Chorleywood. There he set about getting his own meal. For provisions, he carried salt in a little leather sack — and a store of cartridges, for rifle and revolver. A rabbit and a squirrel were collected by two snapshots, before he had roved five minutes from the camping site beside a bright little stream. In a trice, he was back at the place, with a cheerful fire burning.

The squirrels, startled by the noise of the gun, even if they had not known that one of their own kind had been slaughtered, were hushed in the branches above him. Such silence did not please Sandy Sweyn. While he turned the roasting meat on the wood spit above his fire, he raised his head from time to time, uttering little sharp chatterings. Once he gave a cry which exactly imitated the noise of an angry squirrel surprised by another in the harvesting of a rare prize, and ready to fight in its defense.

Presently he had his reward. Half a dozen squirrels slipped out on overhanging branches of the great trees about the spot and commenced to chatter down to him, or to one another, or to the curious blue jay which dipped in and out among the shadows, like a gay jewel.

The jay, itself, came down at last to a lower

branch, and cocked its head to one side while Sandy uttered faint little pipings, imitating with incredible skill the murmurs of a wounded nestling fallen from the nest. The bright, cruel eyes of the jay wandered here and there, in search of the fallen one. At last it looked full at the man, rose with an angry squawk, and hung in the air above the top of the tallest pine. From this height, it seemed to see something behind it in the forest which drew his attention. For it slid through the air to a place where Sandy could no longer see it. Hovering there, it uttered a series of harsh cries. Then its strident voice rapidly grew dim as it flew away.

Before the last of its calls trailed away, Sandy Sweyn had laid aside his roasting spit and caught up his rifle. He knew the ways of the jay, and how that most hated of birds hunts the helpless, haunting those who are strong enough to hunt for themselves. Yonder among the trees was something which had been dreadful enough to startle even the cool nerves of the blue jay. Sandy wanted to learn what it was.

With never so much as a whisper of noise, he melted into the forest, following through it, close to the bank of the stream until his ear, close to the ground, heard the faintest of noises. Hardly a noise, indeed, it was only the soft, soft rustle of pine needles when a heavy weight is brought gently down upon them. It was a weight like the falling foot of a hunting bear.

Prepared to stalk the keenest of all hunters, Sandy Sweyn turned aside and made for the spot from which he had heard the sound by a little semicircle which should bring him behind it. And he smiled to himself as he moved, for he had no doubt that it was a bear, indeed — perhaps some sage, old grizzly, bent on trailing down the scent from the camp fire, and the delicious odor of the roasting meat.

True to the spot, as though he had had the most accurate means of estimating the distance, Sandy Sweyn came upon a narrow gap among the pines. Now he saw the hunter straight before him — not a bear, but an enemy indeed terrible enough to make the blue jay flutter screaming away across the trees. It was a crouched man, stealing forward foot by foot through the trees, his rifle in his hand!

The slow mind of Sandy turned heavily upon this important discovery. What bewildered him was the reason which could have induced the hunter to approach his camp fire with such consummate care and skill.

He was a most expert hunter. Sandy, who had often marveled at the clumsiness of other men in the woods, was all the more amazed by the silken smoothness with which this adept made his way. Once — with a sharp turn of head and body, though soundless as ever — the hunter whirled and showed Sandy Sweyn an evil, suspicious face and two bright eyes bent upon the very thicket where Sandy was hidden.

There was no doubt in the mind of Sandy, now. He knew little of men and their ways. He knew enough of beasts to tell those which preyed from those which were preyed upon. Beyond the shadow of a doubt, this was one who lived upon the prey which he could capture.

It was the more exciting, then, to steal forward along his path. If the hunter was soft in his movements, those of Sandy Sweyn's were like the mere trailing of a shadow. To the ear of owl or bear, the noises he made might have been intelligible enough; but to the human ear, they were nothings.

He gained fast. As the stranger came to the very edge of the clearing and began to straighten to his knees behind a comfortably wide pine trunk, which would give him shelter while he spied upon the place more deliberately, something caught on the butt of his rifle as he drew it up.

Without turning his head, he increased the

pressure a trifle to free it from the root which must have caught in it. He increased the pressure to a tug. Suddenly the rifle was flicked from his grasp. As he turned with a gasp, he saw Sandy Sweyn in the act of rising to his feet with a smile.

There was little real mockery in that smile, rather the natural amusement which Sandy felt in a trail thus followed to a successful ending. To the hunter, it was like a grimace of a fiend. He uttered a faint groan of terror and of rage and jerked the revolver from its holster on his right hip.

No doubt Sandy could have pulled the trigger of the rifle and sent a bullet plunging through the body of this enemy. Such a thing did not even occur to him. He cast the gun itself against the other. The shock of it made the revolver bullet go wide.

When the Colt sent out its second shot, the grip of Sandy was on the gun hand of his foe. The revolver was twisted helplessly to the side.

By loosing his grip on the gun, the stranger managed to free his fingers from a grip which bruised his flesh like the steel of a machine. He drove his fist into the face of Sandy, but it was like striking a heavy India-rubber pad. It did not seem to even jar the head of the other. The next moment the grip of Sandy fell where the teeth of a fighting animal fall — upon the throat of his victim.

There was no resistance. A single pressure, and the hunter hung limp, gasping with wide opened mouth. Sandy trussed him under one arm and carried him out to the open light of the day in the clearing, beside the blazing fire.

He put him down where the stranger could sit on a fallen log, while Sandy squatted on a rock and began to munch his roasted meat, all the while eying the other curiously from head to toe.

He saw the rising of a desperate hope in the eyes of this hunter, marking that there was no weapon leveled at him. Sandy shook his head to discourage flight.

"If you was to run away," said he, "I could run after you and catch you. Or, if I didn't feel like running, I could just stop you with this, d'you see?"

He drew a revolver from his belt. Though it seemed to the stranger that the weapon exploded without more than the most casual upward flash of the eyes of Sandy, yet so carefully was the bullet aimed that before the echoes of the explosion had finished, rushing away among the big trees, there was a rustling and light crashing above them. The limp body of a headless squirrel fell, with a loose thud, upon the bare ground of the clearing.

The hunter buttoned his leathered coat a little more securely around him. Then he shuddered. For, a tenth of a second before, he had actually been considering flight — flight from such a marksman as this! As well might a pigeon strive to flee from an eagle in the high regions of the sky, with cover dreary, dreary miles away.

He fingered his terribly bruised throat and looked downward to the ground.

"What," asked Sandy Sweyn, "might you have against me?"

"Me?" muttered the other. "Nothing."

Sandy shook his head. For the first time he frowned.

"What's your name?" he asked.

"My name is — Coudray," said the other, stiffening just a trifle, as a man will do when he expects that his name will have some effect upon another.

The eyes of Sandy remained blank, except for the cloud of his frown.

"Coudray," he said, "it's not the truth, and I know it. You *have* got something against me. You were hunting me. I ain't smart, but I know you were hunting me!"

Coudray attempted a smile. "It was only a joke," said he. "I smelled the wood smoke. And I thought that I'd sneak up and surprise the gent that built the fire —"

Again the head of Sandy was shaken vigorously in denial.

"I've seen a mountain lion hunting for fun," said he. "I've seen cubs stalkin' each other. And also, I've seen them stalking because their bellies was empty and they wanted food. But you ain't hungry, Coudray, and I ain't ever harmed you none. But still, you was trying to get at me — to murder me, Coudray!"

In all the forest of the Chorleywood, next to Simonides, himself, there was no one man with a reputation like that of Coudray. Whether for strength of hand or ferocity of courage or skill with weapons, he stood by himself, dreaded even by the most fierce of the outlawry. Now he shrank before the youth who watched him.

"Murder?" said Coudray. "What could I want to murder you for?"

"I dunno. I asked you that."

Perspiration poured down the face of Coudray. "Man," he said, "you're talking foolishness."

"I ain't bright, Coudray, but I know when a man hunts to kill. I've never harmed you none!"

Coudray was silent, but his bright, keen eyes wandered desperately back and forth from one side of the clearing to another, hunting for a lie that might serve him, but finding nothing.

To lie to other men was easy enough, but to lie to this strange fellow was quite a different matter.

"If you ain't gunna talk out," said Sandy with a sudden ferocity, "I'll make you talk. When I find that a grizzly is stalkin' me through the woods — I turn back and I kill that bear if I have to trail him for a month! I've done it, and I'd do it ag'in. If a mountain lion comes sneakin' behind me down my trail, I go back and I kill that mountain lion, if I got to foller him right into his cave, in the end. Why should I act any different to you, Coudray?

"You talk, and you talk quick, or I'll finish you now — the same as if you was a bear or a lion! And I'll never have to worry about you afterward. But I'm mighty curious, Coudray. I'm so doggone curious, that I'll let you go. I'll give you your guns, too, before I turn you loose, if you'll tell me why you come out here to hunt for me!"

The hope of life took Coudray by the throat.

"Sweyn," said he, "I'll tell you the truth and the whole truth, if you'll promise, when I'm through, to tell me how you spotted me in the woods!"

"I'll tell you that," said Sandy. "If you'd kept your eyes and your ears open, you would of knowed how I found out where you were.

Now you start talkin'."

"They're set and ready for you in the whole of Chorleywood," said Coudray, talking for his life. "They're waiting for you, and they're gunna get you if you don't turn back. All the reasons that they've got, I dunno. But this here gent, this Peter Dunstan, he's mixed up in it somewhere. What the rest of us know is that Simonides himself has sent around the word that you're to be fixed so's you won't be a bother to anybody — and the white mare is to be took away from you —"

"Elena Blanca!" gasped out Sandy Sweyn. "It's for her that they want me dead? For Elena?"

"I dunno. I tell you what I know. I figured that if they wanted you bumped off, they must have a good reason for it. So I started along and decided that I'd lie out and try to nab you when you come into Chorleywood. Others started along to do the same thing — only it was me that had the luck and spotted you with my field glass a long ways off. So I come down to get at you — and now, tell me what showed me to you?"

Without a word, Sandy Sweyn handed rifle and revolver across to his prisoner.

"You've told me the truth," he said. "I can see that you told me the whole truth. And you're free. But how I found you — why, a blue jay told me where you was. That was all there was to it. You must of heard him talkin' over your head?"

# 17

Sandy Sweyn shifted his camp. His mind was in a complete whirl. All that he had been able to gather from the confession of his captured man was that there was danger afloat for him in the Chorleywood, that Peter Dunstan was connected, in some vague way, with that danger. However, since one man had found him here, he decided that he would be on the lookout with the greatest of care.

When he moved there was no trace left, either of his own footsteps or the footsteps of his two horses, for he took them over a devious way, where he found certain outcroppings of rock that would not show sign of their passing. So, winding up a narrow little ravine, strewn with boulders, he came suddenly, at a turn of the canyon, upon the very man of his search — Peter Dunstan!

One instant of doubt burned in the mind of Sandy Sweyn — and then passed away! When Peter Dunstan came up to him, frankly and happily, shook hands with him, and called him the most wonderful fellow in the world for having captured the mare when so many others had tried and failed, it seemed to simple Sandy that such heartiness could not possibly be linked with dissimulation. He returned the pressure of Dunstan's hand and smiled in turn.

"Aye," said he, "here's the mare. And if you'll turn the dog over to me — why, I'll put a rope on her, and you can take her away, Mr. Dunstan."

Peter Dunstan nodded and cupping both hands at his lips he called loudly: "Chris! O-o-h, Chris!"

Then he hearkened. He called again, listened, and finally he said impatiently: "You'll have to do some training of that fool dog, Sandy, because whenever he gets out of my sight, he runs back to the house —"

"That's queer!" said Sandy meditatively. "Because he wasn't that sort of a dog, when I last seen him. He was the sort of dog that would cotton onto a man and not leave him, unless he was drove away. But you can't tell how a dog is gunna turn out, any more than you can tell how a boy will turn out. They pick up wrong ways. Maybe this'll fetch him." And raising his voice to thunder, which yet had a mellow and inviting note in it, he sent the name of Chris booming across the trees.

Peter Dunstan, remembering how poor Chris lay dead in the grave on the ranch, felt all his nerves stand on end.

199

"He's gone back to the house," he said finally with a note of regret in his voice. "But we'll go up that way and get him for you."

"Aye," said Sandy, "but I don't hardly like it. And I'll tell you why, Mr. Dunstan. There's danger for me here in Chorleywood."

"Danger!" said Dunstan, with a more emphatic enunciation simply because he felt his very flesh crawl. "Danger! Why, lad, you're mad to say so!"

"Listen to what's happened!" said Sandy, "and then you'll agree with me."

He told in detail, word for word, all that he had heard and seen in the Chorleywood, and how he had seen the last of Coudray. By the time he finished, Dunstan had mustered his nerve force again.

"I'll tell you how things are," said he. "There are a lot of bad actors in this neck of the woods. A lot of crooked fellows, Sandy. Regular lawbreakers. Besides, there are some of a good sort who are fiddling around at one thing or another. Some of them have come here to do some prospecting, like a friend of mine whose shack I'm going to take you to. Some of them come here to get the good shooting — like myself. I came up here with Chris for a vacation — to get into the woods, you know — because I never dreamed that you could possibly catch the mare and come back so soon!"

"Vacation!" echoed Sandy Sweyn, opening his eyes with wonder at the rancher. "I never guessed that you was interested in things like that. But the mare wasn't much trouble. She's been used wrong. That's about all that you could say about her. Soon as she got with somebody that understood her, she tamed right down. You see?"

He whistled, and the white beauty danced up to him and snuffed at the hand which he held out to her.

"Here's sixty feet of rope," said Sandy. "When you take her, keep her on this, and give her time to play herself out, if she gets rambunctious."

The very soul of Peter Dunstan ached to get his hands on a rope that was tied to the neck of Elena Blanca.

"Show me what you mean, Sandy," he asked.

Sandy obediently tossed the noose over the head of the little mare and gave the further end into the hand of Dunstan. Behold! The instant that the rope had changed from one hand to the other, Elena Blanca tossed her head and sprang back, bringing the rope taut with a jerk. Had not Dunstan looped it over the pommel of his saddle, it would have been snatched out of his hands. Even as it was, the shock of Elena Blanca's weight made the big horse, caught unawares, stagger. In another moment, there was a fighting, plunging, bucking streak of knotted lightning at the end of the rope, and the hands of the rancher were full.

The voice of Sandy Sweyn rang — and the little white mare ran suddenly to the big, blue roan and crowded against it, her nostrils expanded like transparent crimson silk, her body trembling with her fear and her hate.

"You see," said Sandy, "it'll take a little time. Go along, girl. There's no danger. Steady, honey. We'll come out straight as a string. *He* ain't gunna ride you!"

It seemed to the bewildered Dunstan that the beautiful creature actually understood the words of Sandy. She grew quieter; in another moment she submitted to being led by Dunstan up the valley and then through the broken hills toward the shack of Simonides. What a joy was in the heart of big Peter Dunstan, and the hand which held the rope seemed to him to be closing upon the heart of Señorita Catalina! The picture in his pocket was turning into real flesh and blood.

So they came to the gap in the woods and to the shack of the Greek. There sat Simonides, himself, in front of the door, smoking a vile cigarette.

"Here we are!," called Dunstan. "Here's Sandy and Elena. Have you seen the dog around the house, here?"

"Ten minutes ago," said the ready tongue of Simonides, "the pup was playing with that tin can, yonder, but he saw a rabbit and took away after it —"

"Where?" asked Sandy Sweyn.

"Yonder," answered Simonides. "Between that stump, and the big pine. That's where he disappeared. Come in and —"

"I'll get Chris," said Sandy Sweyn, "and then I'll come back and have a cup of coffee off of you, if you got it to spare. So long!"

He started the big, blue roan toward the indicated spot. Poor Elena began to fight again — but with the choking noose around her neck and the weight of the big gelding in the scale against her, fate was speaking against her, and she was drawn into the corral.

It was the one structure near the shack which was in a state of good repair. There was reason for it since Simonides and his men often had some highhearted horse to confine here. The fence was as tall as it was strong. Elena flashed around it the instant she was loosed from the rope. Then, finding no weak point, she sprang to the center and raised her head in a heartbroken neigh that went shivering far and wide across the forest.

There was silence. Then, out of the distance, came something like an answering echo — the voice of Sandy, calling for Chris through the Chorleywood, while Chris lay dead, so many dusty miles away. Simonides said: "He looks like a simple young fool. What's the danger in him?"

Said the rancher: "He's made Coudray run like a scared dog. That's what he's done already, to-day. And he's coming back, Simonides. When he comes, there'll be trouble — and maybe more trouble than you and I can handle."

Simonides smiled, but then, growing more sober, he whistled. Two men sauntered out from the cabin.

"I made a point of keeping two of the best fellows in the world on hand," said he. "There's 'Dago Lew' — the little chap — and 'Shack' Edwards."

Peter Dunstan took stock of the pair, and truly it seemed to him that he had never before seen two more formidable men than these, standing side by side — Dago Lew, low and broad and powerful; the other, rangy, fast, with shoulders and arms meant for heavy, battering work. Besides, here was his own strength, and Simonides, like a tiger cat!

At last, he smiled.

"You have the men, Simonides, and even

that idiot won't be able to break through. But to-night, all four of us are going to stand watch on the corral."

"Very well," said Simonides. "We won't go to sleep at our posts. Only — what keeps us from telling this Sweyn that the dog must have lost itself in the woods, for that matter?"

"Because if there's a trail, he'll find it. And if he doesn't find it, he'll know that there isn't any trail. Y'understand?"

"Unless he's got the nose of a hunting hound himself, how could he be sure of that?"

"I don't know what he's got. I know what he'll do. By sunset he'll be back here, breathing fire for fair!"

He was not back at sunset time, nor when the yellow moon went up like a disembodied flame through the eastern trees, losing itself in the overhanging pall of the clouds that already shut away the stars. The wind blew soft; it was wet with mist. Now and then a rattle of rain fell on the roof of the shed beside the corral. Still the four watchers could see the ghostly figure of the little white mare as she roamed ceaselessly up and down across the corral.

Another half hour —

"Your man has gone to bed," said Simonides in a soft whisper. "He's lost *his* way and can't come back to us."

"What's that in the shed?" cried the sudden voice of Dago Lew. "Shack, watch yourself!"

The ex-prizefighter had been assigned the task of watching the little shed that opened onto the corral.

Then they heard the loud, absurdly squeaking voice of Shack as he yelled:

"Keep back from me, kid — I don't want to do you no harm. Then take this!"

There was an instant of shuffling, then the sound of a blow of terrible force. It drove the breath in one gasp out of some man's body; then there was a heavy fall.

"Shack has settled your wild man!" said Simonides.

"*No* one man could settle him with bare hands!" vowed Peter Dunstan. "Listen!"

There was a sudden battering and crashing and rending of boards at the back of the shed.

"He's breaking down the wall of the shed to let the mare out!" shouted Simonides. "Dago! Shack! Get at him — guns, boys! Dunstan, come with me — and come fast!"

Dago Lew took the shortest course to get at the seat of the trouble. He came like a bulldog, head down, hungry to get those trained hands of his on the man who battered at the wall of the shed in the darkness, yonder. Once he fixed his experienced fingers on the other —

He sprang into the darkness, and found

there the shining form of Elena Blanca herelf, and beside her the shadow of a man, beating a great gap open. He lurched at Sandy Sweyn and put his arms around the half-wit's body.

There are no words except those of Dago to describe what followed. He told of it long afterward.

"I figgered on squashing the breath out of him. I throwed my arms clean around *his* body and *his* arms. Then I give all my strength to the bear hug, and I feel him sort of sink in in the middle. Then he stops sinkin' in. He turns into India rubber, y'understand? He turned into a bunch of ligaments and tendons like them that run up from the back of a horse. He just spread out and his arms, they give a wiggle like a pair of pythons — and there he was free with his arms. He turned around in my grip as easy as though it was his girl that was hugging him, you'd say. And he fixed one hand under my chin and jammed my head back.

"I felt like I had rested my chin by accident on the head of a piston. After that — he hit me — and that's the reason why my jaw is planted sort of lopsided on my face, y'understand? I didn't feel nothin' much. It just paralyzed me. I went numb. Sitting in the electric chair and having the current turned on — that would be about like getting the wallop from that Sweyn. They call him the half-wit. I tell you, nobody that was a fool could ever of learned to hit like that!"

In short, Dago Lew had leaped into the dark and grappled with his man. Half a second later he lay senseless upon the ground. By this time Simonides and big Peter Dunstan had rounded the outside of the corral and were making for the shed where the wall was being battered down.

But that sound of battering ceased. What they next heard was from the farther side of the corral. The gate had been barred and secured with a padlocked chain. What they heard was the scream of hard wood being torn away from rusted nails. A shriek, a groan, another shriek, and then a section of the ponderous top rail was flung with a clang upon the ground.

Back turned Peter Dunstan to get around the side of the shed. Little Simonides, with a stream of odd-sounding curses flowing from his lips, led the way.

They leaped around the shed's side and into full view of the corral, in time to see a man's body disappear on the farther side of the fence, through the gap made by the tearing down of the upper rail.

Still the fence was high — impossibly high, so it seemed. Peter Dunstan, as he fired wildly toward the spot where Sandy Sweyn had sunk toward the ground, felt that they had won the game, after all, and kept the mare.

Simonides was shooting, too, but he had only a vague direction in which to aim. Sandy was prone on the ground, and in the darkness, he was completely swallowed. Only his voice could guide the bullets as he shouted:

"Elena! Here, girl. Here, Elena!"

"She'll never make the fence even with the top rail down," gasped out Simonides.

There went the little mare, a ghostly streak across the black of the corral. She headed fair and true toward the voice of the man she loved. They saw her slim body arch high into the air — and then the clash as her hoofs struck the rail — the shock as she toppled and sprawled flat upon the ground on the farther side.

"A broken neck — and that's the end of the chase!" muttered Peter Dunstan, groaning.

No — she was up and on her feet like an agile little cat. As she struck forward at a gallop, the two who strained their eyes after her saw a great shadow rise from the ground and leap upon her back. There, flattened along her, Sandy Sweyn drove like an arrow toward the sheltering shadow of the distant trees, where the great blue roan was waiting for him.

# 18

In the long run, everything depends upon Dick in this narrative. The strength and the strange wisdom of Sandy Sweyn, the fiery beauty of Catalina Mirandos, the sage gravity of her father, the big shoulders of handsome José Rezan, the resourceful courage of Sheriff Kilmer, the wind-blown grace of Elena Blanca, and even the freckled face and crooked smile of Peggy Kilmer, could not have brought about the final conclusion of this history, giving it the shaping which it took, without the presence of Dick. It is really necessary to give him a little space in the beginning.

Dick was a setter — a beautiful, red-coated Irish setter — clad in long and curling silk, with the grace of an angel and the mild eye of a saint. He *was* a saint, this dog. Any bird man will tell you that all good setters have been breathed upon by heavenly virtues before ever they enter this world of thorns. Since Ireland is just a little nearer to heaven than any other country — as several million people will agree — it is natural that the Irish setter should have entered just a little more deeply into sainthood than any other breed.

Dick lay on the lawn and listened to the humming of the wind down the valley. That wind brought to him keen scents of the pine trees; from time to time his delicate nostrils informed him that birds were on the wing, but no such birds as he had hunted in green Ireland. He closed his eyes, dropped his head upon his forepaws, and yearned after older and better days.

Then a high, musical voice called, "Ricardo!" He heard it twice before he realized that the name was meant for him. Up he jumped with a guilty start and hurried through the patio, to where his young mistress waited for him in the shade.

He approached her with care, head lowered, tail wagging in the most conciliatory manner. It was true that her voice was wonderfully sweet, but there was a quirt in her hand. He knew of old that that quirt could sting. However, he came at her voice, for still the instinct and the lesson remained firm in his mind that, no matter how strange and cruel some of their ways might be, mankind must be right. It was foolish and very sinful to doubt them. Only children might be shunned, for they did not seem to know that when one's tail is pulled it causes an exquisite pain; also, they are most careless about stepping upon sensitive feet.

"Sit down!" said the girl. "Sit down, Ricardo!"

Ricardo sat down at once.

"Don't look at me as though I were going to beat you!" cried Catalina Mirandos, and she slapped the quirt angrily against her skirt.

A shiver ran through Dick. He gave, in spite of himself, only a tithe of his attention to the face of the girl. The rest of it was concentrated upon the lash of the whip, which he knew could cut so deep. Therefore, he failed to understand when the silver voice commanded sharply: "Come closer, Ricardo!"

Since that order was given in Spanish, Dick did not budge.

"Come closer! I have never seen such a stupid dog! Come right over here!"

Poor Dick merely crouched lower to the ground and wagged his conciliatory tail. The quirt whirled in the air. There was an angry shout from the girl, and Dick blinked his eyes shut in supreme dread.

The whip did not fall upon him, for accident intervened.

"Catalina!" called the voice of a man. She looked askance at her father, who entered the patio.

He was no great lover of animals, but he was a just man, this Mirandos. He said:

"What a devil is in you, Catalina, to make

you beat your dog in this way!"

"I am only trying to teach him a lesson," said she, more angry than ever, "but the fool will not learn."

"Ah, well," said her father, looking curiously at her, "I often wonder, my dear, if you beat him because you wish to teach him!"

"Why else should I?" cried she and stamped her foot.

"Another reason may be that you like to use your power to make him crouch, poor devil! You wish to feel your power over him, just as you wish to feel your power over men. Just as you make men crouch before you and act like cowardly fools, because they want your smiles. Is there not some truth in that?"

Tears of passion sprang into the eyes of the girl.

"It is always this way," said she. "You always find the hardest things to call me, the worst interpretation to put upon everything that I do. You are never kind!"

"There you are!" said her father. "In a temper at the dog because he doesn't understand your language. In a temper with me because you will not listen to what I say!"

"Do I not listen?"

"Yes, but you will not try to understand me. Have you ever sat down by yourself, Catalina, and wondered if you could be wrong about anything? Do you not always tell yourself that you are right, and the rest of the world is cold and brutal if it happens to disagree with you?"

"I am going to my room," said Catalina. "I shall not stay here to be abused."

Her father watched her leave, while Dick crawled to his feet and lay down there, looking humbly up to his new master, thanking him with melting eyes for this kind intervention.

When Catalina got to the door into the house, Señor Mirandos called: "I think you had better stay here, my dear. I have news in this letter that will interest you."

"I don't want to hear your news," said Catalina. "I only know that you hate me!"

Her voice choked with self-pity.

"It is about Elena Blanca!"

At that, she whirled about and came running back.

"Oh," cried Catalina, "what has happened? Has my horse been seen again?"

"The mare is caught," said Mirandos, "and the man who caught her is bringing her here to claim his reward."

"His reward?" said Catalina. "You *will* reward him, father, I know. My beautiful Elena!"

"You forget," said Señor Mirandos, "you promised a reward, yourself. You promised the greatest reward you could give, to any man who could bring back the mare to you."

Catalina leaned a hand against a pillar and blinked her eyes as though a flash of light had dazzled them.

"You promised to marry the lucky fellow," said Mirandos sternly.

"It was a joke!" gasped out Catalina. "It was only a joke, as you know! Who would dare to keep me to such a promise?"

"It is a joke," said Señor Mirandos gravely, "that has kept men hunting for your mare for months. It is a joke that has appeared in the newspapers. It is a joke that has caused poor devils to squander thousands of dollars and their time and hope and labor to catch the horse. No, no, Catalina, it is not a joke at all, but a sad reality!"

"Ah!" cried the girl. "But you do not mean it! You would not give me to some nameless stranger!"

Her father unfolded a letter.

"Listen to this," said he. "It is from Peter Dunstan. You know Peter Dunstan, Catalina?"

"He is the rich rancher," said Catalina eagerly. "It is he, father?"

"It is *not* he who caught the mare," said her father dryly. "It is quite another man, my dear. It is Peter Dunstan who writes the letter, however, and here it is." He read aloud:

DEAR SEÑOR MIRANDOS:

This will let you know what you may have heard already — that Elena Blanca has been caught. But it will tell you what, perhaps, you cannot learn from any person quite so well as from me. The man who caught the mare is named Sweyn, and the only Christian name that is known for him is Sandy. To give you your bad news in a lump — Sandy Sweyn is a hopeless half-wit.

At this, Señor Mirandos lowered the letter and smiled grimly upon his daughter.

"No, no!" said poor Catalina. "You would *never* give me to such a creature as that!"

"Do not try to tell me what I would do, but listen to me, Catalina!"

"I listen, father. But — a half-wit — a dull-eyed, loose-mouthed, stupid —"

"If you had exceptions in mind, you should have made them before you published yourself abroad, my dear. The whole world knows that you have vowed to give yourself to the man who brings the mare to you. And as for me —"

"You are a Mirandos," said Catalina unevenly. "You would never see —"

216

"Hush!" said the rancher. "There is more to follow. You have not heard all the facts which concern this lover of yours!"

He shook out the letter again.

I have known this fellow for a long time, and it is only right that I should give you the advantage of my experience and my knowledge of him. It is not unknown to you, perhaps, that I myself have spent a good deal of time and money to capture Elena Blanca. As a matter of fact, the half-wit was in my employ when he caught the mare. At the last moment, a freak of fancy came over him. He stole her away, and now he is going through the mountains to find her and claim the reward of her hand.

"That is theft!" gasped out Catalina, shuddering with fright. "Something can be done about that. There is a sheriff who —"

"Your promise," said the rancher, "was only to take the mare from any hand that brought her back, and thereafter to marry him, as a reward. If he has stolen the mare, does that make any real difference? No, no! You did not say that it should be the man who secured the capture of the mare. You only specified him who brought her to you. You must remember the facts, my dear, and you must be limited by them!"

He went on with the reading of the letter:

It occurs to me that you may find it worthwhile to attempt to stop this man before he can come to your daughter with the mare and claim that reward of which we know. This would be a tragedy so terrible that I am as much horrified as you can possibly be.

But you will not succeed. He has proved too strong for me, and I am sure that he will prove too strong for you, unless you send out sure marksmen to lie in wait for him, as you would make an ambush for a wild grizzly bear. Believe me, the similarity is not entirely far-fetched!

I remain yours with a thousand good wishes. Instruct me in what I can be of service.

*Peter Dunstan.*

"Let me see!" pleaded the girl.

Taking the letter, she read it through again, letter by letter, printing the awful truth deeper and deeper in her mind.

"But it is *not* possible!" gasped out Catalina. "You could never give me to a beast like this."

Her father was very pale, and his face had become quite drawn. He began to walk up and down the patio. As he walked, he talked — not so much to her as to his own soul.

"You have always been a delight to my eyes, Catalina," said he. "I have always been foolishly proud of your beauty. But I have not given you the sort of treatment that a girl should be able to expect from her father."

"You have always been kind — you will still be kind!" cried Catalina, sobbing.

"Exactly. I have always been kind. I have been too kind, and a child has a right to expect that its parents will give it such discipline that it will be prepared for the coldness of the rest of the world. A girl who has been raised with love only is not prepared for the facts in the world as she will find it. That is cruel. I have been cruel in just this way, my dear! In the meantime, shall I tell you a little truth?"

"Yes, if you will!"

"Very dear as you have been to me, I have been able to see certain faults in you — such as cowardice, cruelty, selfishness, and others of that kind."

"You hate me!"

"No, child; I have a great and foolish love for you. I see these faults in you, but still I hope that they are things which will be lived down. I hope that you will change before you

219

come into full womanhood. That is what hope says, rather than what reason speaks! In the meantime, there are the facts for me to face. On the other hand, there is another thing to which I have given half of my love."

Catalina started erect.

"In that other thing," said Señor Mirandos, "I can see no fault. It is pure and perfect, and I shall keep it so at the cost of everything — my life and yours. It is my honor, Catalina!"

She turned paler than ever, now — and there was a hopelessness in her eyes. The honor of her father was an old, familiar foe to her. No matter of what malleable stuff he might be made, when that sense of honor was encroached upon, she reached a wall of granite that threw back her advances.

"Since the honor of this name has been clean in my hands, I must give you a final warning, my child. I shall not raise so much as a little finger of one hand to prevent the approach of this man who has caught the horse. Once he brings her here, I shall see that you marry him, if I have to drag you to the altar and whip the responses from your lips!"

As he spoke, it was no longer flesh and blood to which she listened, but an abstraction. Honor, indeed!

He turned away from her on his heel, as he said this. Catalina watched him go, filled with horror, knowing that to appeal would be the height of folly.

She ran toward the entrance of the patio, as though she hoped that help might be seen coming to her — or as though the flashing white body of Elena Blanca might be in view. There was nothing except the windy hillside.

She quirted the setter at her feet. "Stupid fool of a dog!" cried Catalina through her teeth. "How can *you* help me?"

# 19

She ran out to the stable. "I want the bay gelding!" the girl cried to Filipo.

"Ah, but, señorita! He is very wild, and he is very fast. And he has not been ridden during these two weeks!"

"That is why I want him, fool! Now hurry, hurry!"

While she waited for the gelding to be caught, she looked down at her clothes. Now that she was in a crisis, she must make her appeal carry the greatest possible force, and she could never do this if she were not looking her best. Back to the house she ran. In her room she scattered all about her and made two hours' work for her maid in five minutes of searching.

At last she had the correct silken scarf, knotted in the proper manner about her waist. She had the proper sombrero on her head, tilted at the smartest angle, with the right feather curling in a crimson streak along its brim. She pirouetted and viewed herself from every side. She needed still something — some touch of color — so she caught up a pair of gaudy emerald earrings and set them in place.

After that, she was content, and with a greater sense of power warming her blood, she raced from the room, still clutching the letter which had brought the fatal warning.

The bay gelding was waiting when she reached the stable. Woe to Filipo if he had taken longer than this to prepare the wild colt! He threw her up to the saddle, for she rode like a boy.

There was need for good riding, here. The bay gelding reared and danced like a very devil, his ears back, foam in his gaping mouth. At length whip and spur rocked him forward. He left the ground with a long leap, and shot off like a greyhound down the valley.

She knew that road well, and it was good that she did, for never did a horse careen over it more wildly than the horse of Catalina on this day.

The first mile was done at the first speed of the gelding. After that it began to falter a little from this terrible pace, and the spurs on the heels of the girl turned crimson as she drove them home. Every second seemed an eternity. In the meantime, there was a savage satisfaction in tearing the last ounce of power from the tormented body of the gelding.

She turned in a cloud of dust through the gateway of another ranch, leaped down, threw the reins at the head of the *mozo,* and rushed into the house itself. A house *mozo* appeared with a smile that turned into a stare.

"Where is José Rezan?" cried Catalina. "*Where* is José Rezan? Instantly! Do you hear? Instantly!"

"He is here. Has your father been hurt, señorita?"

"José! Bring José to me, instantly!"

The *mozo* fled as for life. Presently a door crashed, there was a hurrying footfall, and here was big José Rezan, looking, if possible, more handsome and more huge than ever. He could hardly speak; he was delighted to see this unexpected visitor. He could only extend his hands toward her, but Catalina thrust into those hands the letter which she still carried with her.

"And my father will do nothing!" cried Catalina.

She threw herself into a chair and clasped her hands before her eyes. As for José, he was in a passion of dread when he saw his idol in such a state of mind. Before he had read two words in the letter, Catalina herself was almost forgotten. He read that dreadful missive through from beginning to end, and then glanced back to make sure of the more vital parts. All was vital; all was terrible to him.

He threw himself upon his knees before the girl.

"A half-wit!" cried Catalina.

"Catalina, my dearest, have I your permission to try to stop him?"

"Do you have to wait for that?" cried Catalina. "Do you stay here kneeling and moping while the half-wit is bringing Elena every instant closer to me. If he brings her in, actually, then it is the end! It is the end! Because my father swears like a madman that, for the sake of honor, he will force me to marry this insane man. He will drag me to the altar with his own hands. Do you hear, José Rezan? And still do you stand there and do nothing?"

José Rezan stood still no longer.

Even Catalina was satisfied by the manner in which he rushed from the house; even she smiled with content when she heard his great voice booming in the distance.

Presently José Rezan himself, mounted upon a superb cream-colored charger with a glistening silver mane and silver tail, rushed forth past the house, still thrusting his rifle into the long holster which ran along the saddle beneath his knee. Behind him rode a full dozen of hardy young cavaliers and old men devoted all their lives to the service of the family of Rezan, now ready to live or to die for him.

It was a glorious cavalcade, and as they swept past each cavalier raised his quirt most gallantly to little Catalina — all saving Don José. He bowed low above his saddle and swept his great sombrero toward the ground.

The heart of Catalina was contented.

She mounted the bay gelding again and set off toward her home with greater content in her heart. She told herself that it would be very strange if twelve gallant warriors, who knew the whole countryside as they knew a book, could not find this formidable Sandy Sweyn. No matter how dreadful a fighter he might be, they would crush him.

Catalina looked with much complacence upon this. She felt no twinge of horror. It seemed to her that the impertinence of the half-wit in daring to raise his eyes to her deserved punishment.

She minced down the road, enjoying the picture which she presented to the eyes of others, rejoicing in the mirror of flattery that presented her to herself in every eye which she passed.

Here a cloud of dust swirled by her, and, with a clatter of flying hoofs, Peggy Kilmer, the sheriff's daughter, rattled down the road in front of her, the heels of her mustang tossing up a cloud of dust that showered thickly down upon pretty little Catalina.

Catalina reined in her thoroughbred with an exclamation of supreme disgust. She brushed herself off as well as she could. That was like Peggy Kilmer — to rush about the countryside in this unmaidenly fashion, her hair done into two pigtails, and the pigtails twisted into an ungracious knot at the back of her head, her divided skirt not very much more maidenly than the trousers of an ordinary cowpuncher. Here, for instance, she was galloping off without even a saddle on the back of that ragged mustang — only a blanket strapped on it, and no spurs on her heels as she drummed them against the ribs of the mustang.

No wonder Catalina was disgusted.

As she passed the house of the sheriff, presently, where Peggy was dismounting and dragging the bridle and blanket from her horse, Catalina drew rein a little.

"Hello!" yelled Peggy. "How's things, Catalina?"

She quite missed the answer of Catalina, for she had to leap backward to escape the heels which the mustang flung at her head before he darted away toward liberty.

"I hear your pa bought the Gregory Ranch," said Peggy, dropping her hands upon her hips and turning her freckled face toward the Mexican girl.

"He has bought it, yes," said Catalina. "You must come to see it soon."

"Can't do it to-day! Got the washing to turn out. So long, Catalina. Come in and have a cup of coffee with me some afternoon!"

Catalina could barely force a smile. She was shuddering with disgust as she rode on up the way. It seemed to her that the entire female sex was disgraced by the existence of such a creature as Peggy Kilmer.

In the meantime, like hunting wolves sweeping forward in a swift line, the men of José Rezan rode rapidly across the hills. As they rode, they scattered until there was a great gap between man and man, but never a gap so great that the sound of a rifle shot would not have alarmed the companions to right or to left. There was only one way by which Sandy Sweyn could make his approach to the dwelling of Señor Mirandos. Along that way, which was a deep, broad valley through the mountains, the riders of Rezan were combing every inch of the ground.

One of the horses suddenly fell down heavily in the dust. Apparently he had stepped into a hole in the ground, for it rose almost at once and hobbled a little. When the rider mounted the saddle once more, his mount cantered a stride or two and then paused, shaking its head.

The rider had little patience to expend on his horse. He urged it once or twice with his voice — the quirt rose and fell and the spurs thrust deep. Thus stimulated, the pony bounded forward for a stride or two, and then came to a resolute stop and refused to budge.

There is nothing in the world that will madden a cowpuncher more than a balky horse. This rider fell into a fury at once. His spurs were quickly reddening the sides of his mount when he heard a rushing of hoofs down the slope and, looking up, he saw above him a blue roan mare, moving with gigantic strides. In the saddle was a man who answered in every respect to the description which had been given of Sandy Sweyn.

More than that, in the background ran that delicate beauty among horses — Elena Blanca. There could be no mistaking. That cowpuncher had seen the famous little mare once before, when pretty Catalina Mirandos was in the saddle upon her back, and he had never forgotten.

What he thought of first was to reach for his rifle and try a flying shot at the stranger, but he remembered in that crisis the last warning of José Rezan — that this fellow was a desperate and sure fighter. No one should attempt to handle him without help.

Moreover, the stranger did not seem to be approaching with any hostile intent. He called out in a friendly manner as he came, and he waved his hand. So the vaquero twisted the end of his mustache and waited, trembling with excitement.

When Sandy Sweyn came up, he dismounted at once and went to the puncher with a smile.

"You'll never get that hoss forward like that," said he. "Never in the world! It ain't the whip and the spur that he needs. It's a little talking and a little rubbing."

The vaquero — in the nick of time to keep himself from bursting into heartiest laughter — remembered that this was a half-wit with whom he had to deal. He nodded gravely.

"Talking and rubbing," said he. "I have seen many strange things done with horses, señor, but when they balk I have never seen them persuaded with rubbing and talking. I have heard some grand cursing of them, too, but never anything in the way of language that would get them to move. Nothing but whips — or even a fire built under them!"

"You'll have a chance to see," said Sandy Sweyn. "I may be wrong. Will you get off the hoss?"

The cowpuncher was glad to oblige, for it

chanced that, at this moment, he saw two riders heaving into view, one to his left and one far to his right. He knew that the men of his master would soon be gathering thickly around them. There was the flashing beauty of the white mare to apprise them, even at a distance, of what was there. If only they could send a signal on to the others, in the distance, and so let them know and gather them in silent circle, it would go very hard should Sandy Sweyn escape.

In the meantime, as soon as he had dismounted, Sandy stepped toward the mustang. The latter was now frantic with the pain of whip and spur, and backed off, snorting.

"Come to him, Cleo," said Sandy Sweyn. "Come talk to him, girl. He needs quieting down!"

The vaquero gaped. He was not a superstitious man. He believed that sundry of the saints had been capable of miracles, but he had never seen one that could not be explained by sleight of hand. This, however, was a very different matter, for he could swear that Sandy made no sign to the great blue mare.

Yet, as though she actually understood every word which had been spoken to her, she went instantly to the balking, trembling pony and stood beside it. The mustang leaned heavily against her as if to say: "Stand by me, comrade, and we may yet prove too much for these devils — these terrible men!"

The blue roan touched noses with that frightened mustang. Whatever message it was that she conveyed to him, Pedro, the vaquero, could vow that his horse grew calm. He allowed the stranger to approach with open hand. Pedro would take his oath before any jury in the land that this was a matter without precedence in the history of that broncho.

In another moment the mustang allowed the saddle to be stripped from it. It was turning its head and pricking its ears as it skeptically eyed the stranger.

"Magic!" whispered Pedro, and he crossed himself.

After that, the hands of the half-wit began to roam swiftly over the body of the broncho. Another moment — and there was a sharp squeal of pain from the horse.

"Here it is!" said Sandy Sweyn in triumph. "I knew that it was something near the hocks."

"Señor!" cried young Pedro. "Have a care! That demon of a horse has already put my brother in the hands of the doctor for a full six months. Beware of his heels!"

"His heels?" asked Sandy Sweyn, standing up with a blank eye directly to the rear of the broncho. "Oh, he'll do me no harm. He's feeling happier now!"

With that, he leaned over and began to massage the great tendons and knotted muscles in the back of the pony's right hind leg. So deeply did his finger tips work that the horse fairly groaned with the pain. Its other heel lifted tentatively from the ground half a dozen times, while Pedro looked on in an agony of half-joyous expectation.

There was no kicking. As Pedro declared afterward, even in its pain the mustang attempted to raise its ears from time to time — sure sign that it knew good was being done in its behalf!

In the meantime, Sandy Sweyn talked gently:

"He gave that leg a wrench when he went down. If I were you, I tell you that I should not ride him home. I should simply walk, and let him walk behind you. Better still — to camp out here, to-night, and rub his leg down half a dozen times before morning."

"Walk home — camp out all night — stay awake to rub him down! Ha, señor, do you think that I am taking care of an old mother? This is only a horse, and not a very good one. No, not a very good one at all. He'll take me home to-night or I'll know why, and I'll ask him the question with my spurs. They are sharp enough, if I care to make them talk!"

He laughed rather savagely. Sandy Sweyn

bowed his head and seemed to be lost in thought. He was so deeply lost in it, indeed, that he did not notice beautiful little Elena Blanca come running from the distance to press close to him, her head thrown high, trembling in every limb. He was so lost in thought that he did not hear the creaking of saddle leather as other riders approached him. If he heard, the sounds passed into his subconscious mind and did not affect his consciousness.

At last he said: "If you ride this here hoss, stranger, you're gunna ruin him. If you ride him before to-morrow morning, you will ruin him, sure!"

"Put back the saddle on him, then," said Pedro, growing more confidently insolent as he saw the others pressing nearer to him in a thickening circle. "You've done your part and wasted plenty of my time."

"I'll put back the saddle," said Sandy Sweyn, "but you can't have this hoss to ride until to-morrow morning."

"Can't?" cried Pedro. "Can't? Are you threatening me?"

He reached for his gun with great speed, but he did not make the draw. Light winked at the right hip of Sandy Sweyn, and the long, black body of a Colt glimmered wickedly in the sun as it pointed straight at young Pedro.

"You watch yourself, stranger," said Sandy. "I don't aim at no trouble with you, but —"

His voice trailed away; he had looked up and found a circle of enemies had been thrown around him.

# 20

Sometimes, when more than one gun has secured the drop on him, a desperado, to whom
surrender means eventual death at the hands
of the law, has been known to risk a move
and even to win away to freedom, by diving
at the table which supports the lamp, or some
other trick which throws the others into confusion. There was never a man, since the beginning of time, who could boast that he had
defied and escaped from five leveled rifles,
twenty or thirty yards away, all with a careful
bead drawn upon his heart and head.

Sandy Sweyn stared feebly at these appa-
ritions.

"Where did they come up from, Elena?"
said he. "Doggone me if it don't look like
they had growed up out of the ground in the
last couple of minutes!"

Elena Blanca sidled closer to him as she
heard her name. She had had no doubt, for
her part, from the first moment when she saw
these strangers approaching. She had dis-
trusted them with all of her heart. To her
thinking, there was only one human being who

was really worthy of sublime submission and love. That was Sandy Sweyn. All of the rest were traitors and devils, to be avoided like poison.

"All right, Sweyn," said José Rezan. "Just put up your hands, my friend. I want the guns that you carry, and I want your knife. Move fast, Sweyn."

A smile rose to the lips and the vague eyes of Sandy Sweyn. He lifted his hands above his head.

"If you want money," said he, smiling still, "you'll find that I ain't got none. Money is a thing that I get along without pretty well. But you use a pile of men in your holdup game, don't you, stranger?"

He looked on with admiration.

Half a dozen other riders were now swarming over the edges of the hills, coming at full gallop toward him. José Rezan saw fit to overlook this speech.

"Get to him, Pedro," said he. "And go through him for guns. Be quick, man!"

Pedro obeyed with alacrity. The clothes of Sandy were swiftly searched. One revolver and an old hunting knife were all that were found in his possession.

"And now," said José Rezan, "back up, Sandy Sweyn, and keep clear of us. Valentino, take the blue mare. Get a rope on Elena

Blanca, some of you."

Elena Blanca, too late, seemed to realize that protection for her was not in the power of her companion at this moment. She bolted like a white flash for freedom, but swifter than any horse could dash was the leap of the lariats in the hands of three or four of the vaqueros. In a moment she was plunging blindly in a tangle of lariats.

Valentino, making for the blue roan, had a different problem on his hands. A shrill, sharp whistle from Sandy Sweyn made the big mare leap away, and Valentino lunged hopelessly after her. There she stood, dancing in the distance.

"Watch Sweyn!" called big José Rezan. "Three of you keep an eye on him. The rest of you — except the first two ropes on Elena Blanca — scatter and get the blue roan. We have to have her unless we want Sweyn trailing right at our heels! Get your ropes ready."

They scattered obediently, forming rapidly into a great semicircle, whose horns began to stretch out toward a complete encircling of the big mare. Another whistle came from Sweyn, thin and high as the whistle of a kite and repeated with a rapid tremor.

"Stop that fellow's whistling," called Rezan, "or put a bullet through him. Cut in, lads!"

They went at the blue roan with a willful

rush, but the whistle had been like a precious warning to her. She wheeled away and flaunted off across the valley at a speed which left the horsemen of José Rezan hopelessly to the rear. In a moment or two she was obviously safe from all pursuit.

Old Valentino — the steadiest and the most formidable of all his vaqueros — together with young Pedro, was detailed to remain behind with Sandy Sweyn as a prisoner, while Rezan galloped swiftly away with the rest of his men to carry the white mare to pretty little Catalina Mirandos.

"Take him over to the shade of the trees," said big Rezan. "Give him water when he wants it, and roll a cigarette for him when he wishes to smoke. But see that his hands are tied together, and never take your eyes off him for an instant. I tell you, this man is more dangerous than his dull eye may lead you to think. Watch him till well past noon, and then you may take the rope from his hands and you may ride in. Ride fast, too, for fear lest he should overtake you on the way."

With this he galloped off, and his men followed with only one thing to lessen the speed of their riding — the refractory conduct of Elena Blanca.

Valentino and Pedro, the height of all respect while their master was with them, altered their attitude somewhat as soon as he was out of sight.

They first fastened the wrists of Sandy Sweyn behind him. Then they led him toward the grove of trees. They did not take him into the shade. Pedro felt, in some mysterious manner, that he had been disgraced in the eyes of his fellows by the strange manner in which this fellow had secured the drop on him, even though he was allowed to make the first move toward his weapon. That union of speed of hand together with such vague blankness of eye composed a perfect mystery. Since Pedro could not solve it, he grew vicious.

"The sun," said he to Valentino, "will make this man less dangerous. Let him cook for a while out there, while we watch him in the shade!"

"It may kill him," said Valentino with some caution.

"Well," said Pedro, "do you think that our master will very greatly care for that? Does he really want this man to come in and accuse him of stealing Elena Blanca away from him?"

The logic of this was great enough to beat down the objections of Valentino at once. The pair of them ordered Sandy Sweyn back into the sun with a wave of their drawn Colts.

There was no objection from Sandy. He settled down against a ragged-edged heap of rocks and sat there with the stolidity of an Indian — not a muscle of his face changing.

Pedro settled back in the shadow of the trees.

"We shall see when he begins to moan and beg!" said he, and he laughed until all his glistening white teeth showed.

If you have ever ridden under the summer sun in the mountains, you know with what a force it descends. If you draw rein for hardly more than a moment, that sun begins to eat in through your coat and your shirt. It will scorch the surface of your skin. To sit motionless in that white heat, with the rocks and the sand reflecting it like dull mirrors all around, is more than human nerves can endure.

The face of Sandy Sweyn turned crimson; then it began to grow pale. Perspiration formed on his forehead and ran down into his eyes, stinging them like fire and turning them bloodshot. Valentino shrugged his shoulders in some sympathy with this agony; Pedro laughed aloud.

"This will teach him," said he, "that only fools have gentlemen for their enemies — at least, such gentlemen as José Rezan! It will teach a gringo dog to raise his eyes to such a lady as Catalina Mirandos! And this gringo

— look at him, Valentino! He is no more than a pig!"

If the pig heard, he made no sign. He was working his shoulders steadily, in a patient endeavor to shrug the heat off or to create a little air space between his shirt and his skin. This foolish, patient effort caused a shout of laughter from Pedro, who found it an exquisite amusement.

Only, there was this to be noted — while the shoulders of the wretched Sandy were working ever so slightly and restlessly, his arms were moving behind his back still more. His hands and wrists were steadily tugging up and down. With the tips of his fingers he had located a sharp and serrated rock edge just behind him. He was sawing the rope which bound him, patiently up and down against that stone.

The rock teeth would not bite into the fabric at once; each strand had to be frayed and then rubbed thin. Finally it parted, shred by shred.

"I think that he is getting sick, Pedro. Look at his face!"

To be sure, it was very pale and haggard, and the lines sank deep.

"He is like a balky horse," said Pedro. "He will not stir or complain. However, I shall see how he is!"

He stepped forward and, with the loop of

his quirt dropped under the chin of the prisoner, jerked the head of Sandy suddenly and brutally back. His hat fell off, and his eyes looked up into the face of Pedro.

Valentino laughed heartily, consumed with mirth at this prank of his companion.

"His eye has not the look of the eye of a dead fish, as yet," said Pedro, returning with a smile to the cool of the shadows. "But we will let him cook for a while with his hat off. That may hurry the boiling! That sun has an edge like a knife. It bites through my coat!"

Sandy Sweyn sat without a hat, sweltering in that cruel sun, but never changing a muscle of his face in acknowledgment of the increased torment. It was not torment which he had to crowd back from his eyes and mouth. It was a savage exultation and an expectation of revenge, for now the rope was deeply cut.

He worked harder than ever.

"He is fainting, Pedro!" exclaimed Valentino at last. "See how he sways! You see that his white skin was never meant to endure the full sun of the day. See how he sways!"

"Gringo!" said Pedro. "Will you beg for help now? Will you crawl on your hands and your knees, or will you wriggle like a worm, if we let you come into the shade?"

He raised the quirt with an angry snarl.

"Will you speak, pig?"

He got no answer. Therefore, Pedro lurched a long stride forward, swinging the quirt high. The thought of how that quirt would feel, swishing down upon the scorched shoulders of the prisoner, forced an irresistible temptation to Pedro.

This hurried the process which had been carried on with such patience. It forced Sandy Sweyn to place the knuckles of his hands together and then to buckle the wrists outward. Under that tremendous strain, the last strands of rope parted with a snap, like a parting cable. The thick arms of Sandy Sweyn swung far out from his side, free!

Ah, Pedro, however swiftly you have leaped and sidestepped in your wildest dances, be far faster now, for there is need! Pedro leaped, you may be sure, with a scream of terror, forgetting his raised whip and clawing at the revolver at his belt.

He was pulled down from below. Fingers stronger than the talons of an eagle laid hold upon his ankle and wrenched him to the ground, where his back struck with such force that all the air was knocked at once from his lungs and the revolver shot far away across the sands.

Valentino, filled with amazement and horror, whipped out his own gun and leaped to his feet. As he rose, the gringo rose also, with the helpless body of Pedro in his arms. Where could Valentino shoot, without sinking a bullet into the body of his compatriot?

Then a miracle happened. The body of young Pedro shot backward through the air straight at Valentino's head, propelled from the inhumanly strong hands of Sandy Sweyn.

There was no more than time for a partial dodge; one of the wide-flung arms of Pedro struck full across the face of his friend.

Valentino was man enough to rally in spite of this handicap. He fired, but he was still more than half blinded by that unexpected blow, and before his eyes cleared the wrist of his gun hand was in a grip that made the bones bend. The Colt dropped from his numbed fingers.

Sandy Sweyn gathered his captives together, one in either arm. Then he shifted his grip. In his left hand he gathered the long hair of their heads and held them so. With his right, he went leisurely through their pockets.

He said nothing as he worked, but he proceeded with care. Nothing escaped him. Not even the brown papers of Valentino's cigarettes. Even these were extracted and tossed into a careful little pile.

Then Sandy Sweyn stood up. Still holding them by the hair of the head, he dragged them backward to the spot where their horses stood.

"Kill me at once!" cried Valentino. "After such shame, I do not wish to live!"

Sandy Sweyn only laughed, and that laughter made Pedro scream again. He wrapped his hands around the leg of Sandy.

"Señor!" he gasped out. "I swear that I shall be your servant. I shall always —"

"Peace!" cried Valentino. "Peace, cowardly dog, because if we live I shall slit a throat that shames our whole race. Will you beg — after what we have done to him?"

Pedro begged no more; he had fainted in utter anguish of spirit.

In the meantime, from their own saddle-bows, two rawhide lariats were detached. With these Sandy tied them, back to back and heel to heel. He secured their heads together by knotting their long black hair — an ingenious device which pleased Sandy. After that, he tied them to the rocks. Then he stood up and regarded his work.

"So!" said Sandy Sweyn. "You will toast a little, also. Come, Cleo!"

At his call, the blue roan mare, which had lingered not far off all of this time, came sweeping in to him with a joyous whinny.

He leaped into the saddle and regarded the prisoners with another critical stare. The sun was hanging at its hottest pitch, and every instant of their exposure would be a keen agony. Unless they died of panic, before very long the setting sun would throw a shadow from the pines toward them. For that shadow, how eagerly they would wait!

These things were noted by Sandy Sweyn, and he nodded his head and smiled to himself. Although he felt in his heart a loathing for all humans that he had ever seen, he could not bring himself to downright laughter.

He turned loose the two mustangs, also. From the back of the lamed horse of Pedro he removed the saddle and the bridle with care. He nodded while he watched it hobbling slowly off, throwing its head as the strain came at each step upon its injured leg.

Quiet and the heat of the sun would restore that leg by the next morning, thought Sandy Sweyn. He turned for a last look at the vaqueros. Valentino was silent, as ever, composing himself.

"Water!" screamed Pedro, who had revived. "A little water, kind Señor Sweyn! A little water!"

The deadly snarl of Valentino interrupted him. "Puppy! It is not ten minutes since you half emptied your canteen. Be still, or I shall find a way to kill you sooner than the sun would do that good work!"

The voice of Pedro broke into a wild sobbing. Sandy Sweyn, with a shudder of disgust, turned his back and sent his horse cantering swiftly up the valley in the pursuit of the troop which had carried Elena Blanca away.

He thought of the little white mare and the injustice of the men. As for Catalina Mirandos, he hardly thought of her at all. She was to him a strange mystery. Why men should hunt the little mare for the sake of Elena's swift-footed self was explicable. Why they should wish to hunt her merely for the sake of a woman, he could not understand. He had been filled with only a mild curiosity to look upon the face of Catalina.

# 21

In riding up the valley Señor Rezan had not neglected to place final outposts, two reliable men. Where the valley narrowed to a simple gorge they were instructed to wait among the rocks, so that, if Sandy should escape from his guards, they could block his way from these final points of vantage.

When he had established these final marks of safety, Rezan hurried on. Finally he reached the Casa Mirandos.

Others had seen him coming. They had heard the trampling of the hoofs of his horses. They had looked out and seen the famous beauty of Elena Blanca, and in that single picture they were able to read a story which told them that the long chase was over, at last. The most romantic incident that had ever taken place in those old mountains was now preparing for its last act. They tumbled out and mounted their horses in haste to follow.

The procession passed toward the house of Mirandos. When they arrived at the patio, Don José would have kept the others back, but there was a great roar from all their voices:

"We will have Catalina Mirandos come down to the patio! Where is she? Let her come. Señor Mirandos, bring down your daughter to the patio!"

Señor Mirandos would have been glad to escape from such a necessity. He would have sent Catalina closely to her room, to stay there until the mob was gone, for he was not one to enjoy having his daughter stared upon.

But how could he control her? The chance of being looked at was so charming to our Catalina that the roses blossomed at once in her cheeks. She was at her glass only long enough to crowd a red rose into the shadows of her hair. Then she was flying down the stairs and dodging past the sedate form of her father.

Yet when she slipped out into the patio, it was with the shrinking step of a deer frightened by the hunter from its covert. The color which vanity and haste had put in her cheeks appeared the blush of maiden modesty. Oh, wise Catalina! So well did she manage it that a veritable shout went up from the crowd, not only from her Mexican compatriots, but from the true Americans, also, who had ridden up to join in the formal triumph of big José Rezan.

Then she saw Elena Blanca and started forward with a glad cry. You would have thought that Elena was really something more than a mere peg upon which the notoriety of Catalina Mirandos had been hung. The men grinned in pleasant understanding. It was, of course, the general idea that Catalina was so terribly fond of the mare, and the white mare was so terribly fond of her, that when that beautiful companionship was interrupted Catalina could not help but offer any reward in the world to the lucky man who would bring back the mare to her.

Elena Blanca, like the little devil that she was, now threw a monkey wrench into the idyl by beginning to rear, paw the air, and prance around when she saw her mistress, acting as though her one passionate desire was to smash the fair Catalina to a pulp. Catalina had no idea of letting herself come too close to the white devil.

"See what they have done to her! They have made her into a savage beast!" cried Catalina, with tears in her eyes — she always had tears at her command. She clasped her hands together.

As for the men, they were busy controlling that little white flash of a mare. There was only one pair of eyes which remained fixed upon Catalina. Glancing down toward the rear of the crowd, she encountered the quizzical smile of Peggy Kilmer, the sheriff's daughter.

The flush deepened upon the cheek of Catalina.

She knew that Peggy understood. What men could never understand, the quick glance of a woman could unravel. Catalina knew that her mystery was open as the day to the glance of this girl. She sighed, turned a little away, and wished that the freckled face of Peggy Kilmer were any place in the world other than here.

Now came tall José Rezan and stood before her, looking stupidly guilty and ill at ease. She drew José with her into the house of her father. The crowd gave its last shout as they disappeared together. Inside, they encountered the wicked tongued Señor Mirandos himself. He said:

"So she is taking the bear to escape from the lion. Is that it, José?"

His daughter made answer with an ugly look, and then she drew José on to the living room and sat him down beside the great open window.

"José, my José," said she, "what a hero you are! And how did you manage to do it?"

"We met him and took Elena from him by force," said José, "and that was all that there was to it."

"He was not so terrible, then, as a fighter? There was no one really hurt?"

252

It might have seemed, to a discriminating eye, that there was a shade of disappointment in the eye of the girl as her lover answered: "No one was hurt. He looked merely simple. One could see that he was a half-wit. He looked like a man only half awake."

"But how could he have captured Elena, if he has only half of a normal man's wits?"

"Because he rides the fastest mare that I ever saw, and the strongest. We tried to catch her — to keep him from following us. She simply laughed at us. I have never seen such speed!"

"Then he *will* follow?" exclaimed the girl. "Oh, José, be careful. You are all mine, now, and you must take the greatest care of yourself!"

José could not help smiling, remembering the rope which bound Sandy Sweyn and his two guards posted in the valley.

"There is no fear," said he. "You shall not see him here. He will not follow!"

"And yet," said Catalina, "I can hardly believe that he may not find a way — if he had wits enough to capture Elena, you know!"

In one thing more José felt himself enormously lucky. When he pressed for the wedding day, Catalina was willing to waive a long preparation. It might be to-morrow, she said, and the face of honest José Rezan lighted with a consummate joy.

As the day was turning toward the dusk he rose to depart. Before he reached the door of the Casa Mirandos there was a rattle of hoofbeats outside in the patio, then a babbling of voices at the door.

The door opened. A man staggered in before them, his face drawn, his head tied in a crimson rag.

"Carlos!" cried big José Rezan. "What has happened?"

"Sandy Sweyn!" gasped out the other. "He has broken through us!"

José Rezan pushed him into a chair and brushed the chattering servants from the room.

As for Catalina, exclamations of pity and of distress poured from her lips. As she hurried to bring wine, warm water, and to make a clean bandage for the head of this Carlos, it seemed to that hardy vaquero that she was an angel of mercy, sent from heaven to relieve the woes of man. In the eye of the girl there was a profound satisfaction.

Sandy Sweyn, seeing that he was a half-wit and a fool, of course, should not be permitted to claim the reward which she had offered to him who brought back the little white mare. At the same time, she was consumed with curiosity about him.

Of all the cavaliers who had ridden forth to perform this great feat, it had remained to this mysterious Sandy Sweyn to conquer. It seemed hardly right that he should be caught like a foolish bird in a net at the very moment when he had almost brought the horse back to her! It seemed very wrong, indeed.

When she went up to her room that night there were only two things of crowning importance that remained in Catalina's imagination.

Neither of them had to do with José Rezan and the fact that she had most impulsively promised to marry José on the following day. Nor was it her concern at the anger and contempt of her father when Señor Mirandos had learned of the hasty decision of his child.

José Rezan had so often been in her life, and out again, that she was used to him; she was also used to the angers of Señor Mirandos himself. There were two new features in her history that seared her thoughts.

The first of these was the keen glance with which Peggy Kilmer had looked straight through her armor of elaborate affectations to the truth about herself. It was a new and almost an unheard-of thing for Catalina to feel that any human being had looked in upon the shadowy inside of her existence, with all its turmoil and noisy shallows.

She hated Peggy Kilmer for having seen so many things so well. She hated the freckle-faced girl for the superior power which enabled her to smile at what she saw in Catalina. We chiefly rage, not at those who attack us in passion, but at those who glance aside at us in scorn. She vowed chiefly that she would be avenged upon Peggy Kilmer for knowing too much.

However, Peggy was not even the major half of her thoughts. There was another person looming larger and larger. That was Sandy Sweyn. Surely his actions on this day had hardly been like the actions of a half-wit! He had twice handled two fighting men as though they were silly children — for Pedro and Valentino had been found and brought in.

With eyes half closed, she pondered over this figure, who lay more in a world of dreams than in the world of reality — a half-wit with the strength of a giant and with a craft in fighting which turned even such sturdy vaqueros into mere puppets and children.

What roused her from her ponderings was a mere whisper of sound at the farther casement, on the other side of the room. Catalina looked up in time to see the figure of a man swinging through the open window and dropping lightly to the floor — so lightly that, in spite of his bulk, his feet made no sound whatever as they struck.

It brought Catalina instantly to her feet. It was characteristic of her that in ordinary times she chose to be excessively feminine, while in a crisis she was as cool as a young tigress. She sprang back toward the door, and she laid a hand upon the knob of it, ready to flash away to safety at the first movement of the stranger. She lingered for an instant, and from her dress she plucked forth a little Italian stiletto, delicate and deadly, shaped to a long needle point. In spite of her soft beauty, this Catalina was a true daughter of the desert, practiced in its ways.

She knew him instantly by the descriptions which others had given to her of him. She knew him by the deceptive appearance of softness and the real power which underlay it. She knew him by the deft quiet in which he had climbed the smooth side of the house and swung into her room. No leopard could have been more dexterous in the hunting of his prey. She knew him, above all, by the dull and handsome features, that unlighted eye, the color of sand, which seemed blurred and lost under lashes of the same tone.

Staring at her beauty, the eyes of Sandy Sweyn opened a trifle, and there began slowly in their deeps a tremor of golden fire that waxed and waxed until, at last, it was flaming at her.

It seemed to Catalina Mirandos that he stood straighter, his head raised, and a faint smile of joy stirred his mouth. What a fire was this she had lighted in him! The beautiful form of Dick slipped in from the outer room, sensing trouble though there had been no sound even to reach his sensitive ears. He sprang in front of his mistress like a true hero, ready to do his duty. When he faced the stranger, a little tremor ran through Dick, and presently he crouched on the floor and was staring up with wonder at Sandy Sweyn, beginning to brush the floor with his silken tail.

Danger in this man? Catalina was no fool, and she knew that where her Ricardo could love so quickly there must indeed be something lovable. She, looking wide-eyed upon the stranger, began to see what those qualities might be — endless strength, endless simplicity, endless trust, endless power to worship. She knew that she was, at this moment, seeing Sandy Sweyn as no other person had ever seen him. She had been able to strike a great fire which hitherto had never flamed, and which might never go out. It was an exquisite flattery, so subtle that it was beyond words.

When he spoke it was as directly as a child.

"I came to bring back Elena Blanca, but

they stole her from me. Then I wanted to see you, so I came here. You are not afraid of me?"

"I am not afraid!" said Catalina.

She saw the silken softness of her voice send a tremor through him. He passed across his eyes that hand which had beaten down so many men this day.

"I've been walking in a dream!" said Sandy Sweyn. "But now I'm awake. I never knew that a woman could be like you, Catalina! May I come closer?"

She was too excited to answer. Perhaps it looked like fear to Sandy; to the girl it was really only the thrilling joy of her power that moved her, and wonder at this strange creature which had come to her hand. She saw him move a step nearer, and another. He stood just before her, and now his eyes plunged deep in her great black eyes.

Dick stood up, but the stranger had no eye for him. He made a vague gesture toward her, and Catalina shrank a little; yet she did not step back. All that he touched was her hand, and he raised it to his cheek, to his lips.

Then he stood straight before her again, and her hand had fallen away. It was unlike all that other men had ever done in her presence. It was a strange mixture of the worship of a child and the love of a man. There was such joy in him that he was almost laughing.

"I listened at the window below," said he. "I know that Don José is to marry you to-morrow. Tell me, Catalina, do you love him?"

She had no words. A sort of trembling weakness spread through her body and rose to her throat and closed it.

"Ah," said Sandy Sweyn, "I knew that you did not! Forget him, then, because he does not exist!"

He stepped back to the window. One gesture swung him out. He turned to give himself a last look of her, with the expression of one drinking the wine of the gods. Then he was gone. Only then Catalina realized that she had not spoken a word since his entrance, except: "I am not afraid!"

It was not much to say, yet she felt that she had conquered a new world.

She ran hastily to the window to stare after him, but he was gone in the blackness beneath. Not so much as a whisper came back to her.

Dick, standing at the casement, also, with his paws resting on the edge of it, looked down also, and whined as though his heart were breaking to be out.

# 22

Those who listened through opened doors and windows heard a man ride singing down the valley that night. There was never a voice so great and so ringing, they thought. They hurried outdoors, but all that they saw was a vague figure, under the dim moon, riding down the road. Even when they stood in the open, they could not distinguish the words of that song or the language of the singing. The tune itself seemed to be a merely inarticulate overflowing of joy.

When the rider came to the house of Sheriff Kilmer, the wind blew tidings of food to him. The sheriff had returned late this night from a long ride, and his daughter had barely set the meal before him on the table. An instant later there was a knock at the kitchen door, and Peggy Kilmer opened that door on a man with wild yellow eyes and long, thick sand-colored hair.

"I'm hungry," said the stranger. "Will you feed me?"

The black cat leaped up from the warmth behind the stove and ran into a far corner of the room, where it cowered in the sheltering blackness.

Peggy Kilmer had never been afraid of men, any more than had little Catalina Mirandos, but from a different reason by far. Catalina knew that they were helpless in the power of her smile. Peggy Kilmer considered that they were all her brothers.

Nevertheless, she was afraid now. Never had the night showed to her such a person as this. Yet her duty was clear before her. In the mountains, when food is asked for, it must be given even by a miser. She was very glad that her father was here with her, sitting at the kitchen table with his supper spread before him. She cast at him a single glance which was enough to show him that here was something extraordinary. The sheriff leaned forward a little and loosened the revolver in his holster.

What he saw, as the stranger stepped through the doorway, made him come to his feet.

"You're Sandy Sweyn," said Kilmer.

The stranger turned on him with such a sudden lightness of body that the sheriff started again; when he met the yellow light in those eyes he caught his breath.

"I'm Sandy Sweyn," said the stranger. "Who are you?"

"Kilmer is my name. I'm the sheriff of the county, Sweyn."

"Good," said Sandy Sweyn. "Have you got chuck here for an extra hand, partner? I've never ate with a man-sized sheriff before!"

He laughed in an odd, joyous way that made Sheriff Kilmer, for an instant, suspect that his guest had been drinking.

"Sit down," said he, "but before you sit down I have to say that I have an idea that I ought to put you under arrest, Sweyn. You're accused of having attacked four men, to-day. And one of them is badly hurt. There's no charge against you, and that's why I'm a little in doubt."

"We'll talk it over while I eat," said Sandy Sweyn.

The sheriff nodded. "Put on another steak in the frying pan, honey," he said to his daughter. "Excuse me a moment, Sweyn. I have to telephone."

As he passed from the room he heard Sandy Sweyn saying: "Never mind the new steak. I smelled beans as I came in."

The stranger went to the stove and, taking from it the great, blackened bean pot at the back of the fire, he sat down contentedly with a huge iron spoon.

At the telephone, behind closed doors, the sheriff was speaking rapidly and softly. "Is this you, Rezan? I have news for you. Sandy Sweyn is in my house. He stopped to ask for his dinner. Now, Rezan, never mind exclaiming. What I want to know is if you are preferring any charge against this man?"

"No!" said Rezan instantly. "He's more likely to prefer a charge against me. You understand, don't you, sheriff?"

"I understand," said the sheriff. "You stole a horse from him, and he raised the devil with four of your men. One of them is still out of his wits, and another is dangerously hurt. I don't know where the balance lies, but I suspect that it lies against Sweyn. You don't want to do anything?"

"Not a thing!"

"Then I make one suggestion."

"What's that, sheriff?"

"Keep a gun under your pillow when you sleep to-night. I've never seen such a queer-acting fellow, and he may be up to mischief."

"I'll take your advice, sheriff, and thank you."

"One thing more. Can you tell me why people call this man a half-wit?"

"Why, sheriff, there was never any doubt as to the reason for that. He's different from other people. And his dull eye, if nothing else —"

"Dull eye?" asked the sheriff. "I've never

seen a bright one, then! But I've sent you a warning, Rezan!"

"A thousand thanks. I'll be on my guard. But I wish nothing but good luck to this fellow. Has *he* made a charge against me?"

"Not a word, but it may come, later!"

The sheriff returned to his kitchen, and there he found Sandy Sweyn deep in the contents of the bean pot, talking to Peggy Kilmer at the same time. As for his Peggy, he had never seen her so flushed nor so pretty, sitting in the window, swinging her heels. In the instant that her father had been away, she seemed to have pocketed all of her fear of this stranger.

"Look, dad!" said she. "Old Tabby has found a friend! Never knew her to *look* at a man before!"

The sheriff could hardly believe his eyes. Black Tabby sat upon the broad shoulder of Sandy Sweyn, her tail wrapped around her forepaws, purring in blissful content.

Every movement of the spoon she regarded with much interest, as though this were a sort of food that even she could enjoy! The sheriff was in awe when he sat down. In years of effort he had never secured the confidence of that mysterious cat. No wonder, then, that the heart of his daughter had been touched!

"But," went on Peggy, as though her father

were not there at all, "if you live all alone in the woods most of the time, what do you do for company? I should think that you would die of loneliness!"

"Oh," said Sandy Sweyn, "I never lack for company. You see?"

He whistled, and instantly, through the open kitchen door, the head of a magnificent blue roan was thrust. She whinnied no louder than a whisper and pricked her ears at her master.

"You see," said Sandy Sweyn, "that I have company!"

"I see. But very queer company, most people would call it! And only your horse?"

"There's a bear," said Sandy, "that drops in on me in the summer. And we often hunt together. There is more fun in going fishing with a bear than with a dozen men, I suppose."

She started to laugh, but when she saw that he was in earnest it did not occur to her to doubt. The sheriff himself felt no question in his mind. To the man with those blazing eyes and that inward joy all things seemed possible.

"But to-night," said Sandy, "I've got a different slant on things. I've waked up to the fact that there's something besides animals in the world. Girls, for instance. I never really saw them before!"

He looked straight at Peggy Kilmer and

laughed — not an insulting laugh, but as though he were flooded with such happiness that it had to find some expression. A flare of color went up the cheeks of Peggy — and she looked rather guiltily and impatiently at her father, for all the world as though she wished him out of the way! The sheriff was amazed. It was not in the cards for his daughter to pay more than the most casual attention to young gentlemen — except to include them as sort of secondhand brothers.

Sandy Sweyn was enlarging on the point. "Look at her!" said he. "I've tried out men and found that most of them are hounds. But the girls are different. There's something in her that no man could ever have. Will you see the color in her cheeks, sheriff, and how her eyes sparkle? Why, I tell you that it makes me happy only to look at her!"

The sheriff started to frown. Suddenly it dawned upon him that this was not brazen boldness, but merely a true naïvete such as no other man in the world possessed. Peggy herself seemed to know the honesty of the stranger; certainly her blush was not one of displeasure.

The iron spoon grated on the bottom of the iron pot. The steaming cup of coffee was poured at a single gulp down the capable throat of Sandy Sweyn. He stood up and laid Tabby on the floor.

"Adios!" said Sandy Sweyn, standing at the doorway and smiling back at them. He turned to the girl. "I'd like a lot to come back, some time, and talk to you again, if I may."

"Sure," said Peggy Kilmer. "There's nothing to keep you from it, I suppose."

"Because," said Sandy, "if I was to talk to you a little longer, I think that I might be able to find out why it is that you make me so happy. You understand? Adios!"

He was gone into the night.

The sheriff stared after him in complete bewilderment.

"Look at that confounded cat!" said he. "It's following Sweyn, or trying to!"

There was no answer from his daughter. When he stared at her, he saw that she was peering far off at things which he could not see and which, he guessed, he never could entirely understand. The dream was in her eyes. Her fingers twisted idly together. A faint smile touched her lips.

"I never saw another fellow like him!" said the sheriff.

"Nor I!" said Peggy Kilmer.

"Fresh talking, but not really brassy. No manners, either, and yet he didn't seem to need 'em."

"Manners?" cried Peggy. "What was wrong with them?"

"What was wrong?" gasped out the sheriff. "Why, honey, he didn't take his hat off for a minute while he was in the house!"

"I didn't notice," said Peggy.

"And how much did he thank us as he left?"

It seemed that Peggy was slipping back into her dream again, and she made no answer. Presently she stood up from the low window sill and left the kitchen, and the sheriff, frowning into his cup as he stirred the sugar into the coffee, realized that Peggy was a woman, after all. Soon she must leave him!

# 23

In the house of big José Rezan, he was as good as his promise to the sheriff. He searched his mind to pick out the men best qualified to serve him. First, he selected two stout and watchful vaqueros and bade them keep constantly roving about his house. To sharpen their watchfulness, he murmured one word only: "Sweyn!" That was enough.

Then he remembered two men who were both dreaded and despised by his vaqueros, two surly giants, black of brow and dark of face, who had recently come down from the mountains and taken employment with him, tending his flocks of sheep. He had sold his sheep. Now they waited for the purchase of his new flock; they waited in sullen silence, speaking to no man, communicating even to one another by signs only, most of the time.

Vicente and Lorenzo stood, thick of neck, with crooked wrists from much hard labor which they had done in their lives. In such hands as these, gun or knife would be out of place. Such hands were not meant for adroitness and agility, but to crush with the seizure. Such hands were made to break and to rend. They were like the paws of bears.

He put a stout cudgel in the hand of either man.

"Now," said José Rezan, "here is the corridor in front of my room. The window of my room is barred, and no man can come through it. I expect that an attempt may be made upon my life to-night. To-morrow I am to be married, and such great happiness, my friends, seems almost too much for me to look forward to. Therefore, I put my life in your hands, and I give you a great trust."

They heard him without a sound, and they went to the ends of the halls, where they were concealed in the thickness of the dropping shadows. Rezan knew that there would be no danger; eyes that watched over his flocks by day and night would not close in this greater time of need! He went to his bed and slept like a child, secure that all would be well.

When he wakened, it was to hear a slight groaning sound in his room. He sat upright; again he heard the groaning, and this time he made out that it came from his window. Presently he recognized that awful sound as the noise of iron bent with a terrible force against the stones!

Rezan could hardly stir for a moment. Then, against the stars, he saw the head and shoulders of a man thrust into his chamber. He tried to shout — but the result was a scream, rather than a call for help. He jerked the revolver from beneath his pillow and fired. Even as he pulled the trigger, he knew that the shot had flown wild from his trembling hand. The next instant, the black form had slipped through the window and dropped to the floor of his room.

In the corridor, outside, there was a stir of great voices. Vicente and Lorenzo knew that danger was there, and they were beating against the door to come to his aid — that door which he had so madly locked the night before, secure in the strength of the iron bars that guarded his window!

In a moment, unless his hands could be steadied and unless he could shoot straight, the hands which had bent the iron at his window would be at him, breaking and rending!

Another scream rose from the throat of José Rezan, as he fired again and again! But his nerves were shattered. Through the dark a form leaped at him like a cat, which springs in and dodges with a swerve as it springs. A hand shot past his gun arm; a frightful grip was laid upon his wrist. Then a blow struck full against his face.

He fell with a faint moan and knew no more. That instant, however, the door of his chamber fell with a crashing. The two giant shepherds were rushing in to the defense of their master. What they found was a confused tangle of shadows upon the floor. Vicente struck, and his master groaned like a dying man beneath the stroke!

They threw themselves into the struggle with their bare hands, and therein they made their mistake. With the clubs they could have felled oxen. Under their hands they felt a lightning and an animal power, shifting from their grips. When they strove to sink their fingers into the flesh of this man, it turned instantly to India rubber beneath their touch. Their fingers slipped harmlessly away. In the meantime, dreadful hands laid hold upon the two brothers.

The house had been roused by this time. The two vaqueros from the outside were speeding in. The stout *mozos* had tumbled from their beds and come, knife and gun in hand, in a swarm.

Sandy Sweyn heard the rushing of the many feet. Intent as he was upon the dreadful work which lay before him, he knew enough to understand that this was the limit of his daring. He must turn and strive to get away, if he wished to live.

He rose from three prostrate figures and rushed to the door. There he met a flood of struggling, shouting men, and he clove through them like a hot wedge through butter. He had scooped up one of the clubs of the two brothers, and before the very shadow of his stroke the *mozos* gave way. The tangle of their forms as they strove to flee from him blocked the efforts of more valiant fellows.

Perhaps Sandy would have come unscathed from this strange battle had it not been that Vicente had risen from the place where he fell. His left arm was broken by the terrific wrenching grip of Sandy Sweyn, but his right arm was intact. In that arm there was the strength of two.

Besides, he was nerved by a frenzy of excitement, now. As he plunged for the door, he gathered up the club which he had let fall when he leaped to the help of his fallen master. Armed, he leaped with a shout into the hall. With his broken arm swinging and hanging loosely at his side, he sped forward. His footing was upon fallen men more often than upon the floor.

Sandy Sweyn heard that shout and guessed at the flying danger behind him. As he turned, his foot slipped. He dropped to one knee and, before he could rise, the blow was driving at his head. He reared the club as a guard; in his hand it was like a shield. Had there been power enough in the wood, he would have been saved, but the blow of Vicente's club snapped the bludgeon which Sandy Sweyn raised to meet it, and descended on his head.

What seemed to Vicente himself the greatest miracle of all was that the stranger was able to rise even after this blow. To be sure, its force had been partly checked by the guard which he had raised against it. Even so, there seemed enough sheer weight remaining to have broken the head of any normal man.

Sandy Sweyn was no normal man; even he was staggered. He rose to his feet and lurched at Vicente, but half of his power was stolen from him, and his head rang with the effects of that blow.

They could close on him now, and close on him they did, like valiant bulldogs pulling down a bear. By the grace of chance no ready knife was sheathed in his body, but he was fairly swathed in stout ropes. By the time his senses had cleared, his arms were almost helpless.

They stood about him, panting and gasping with their efforts. Seeing the great rise and fall of his breast as he breathed himself; it seemed to those awe-stricken men of the Casa Rezan as though the stranger would snap even the strong ropes that bound him.

Some of them guarded him closely with ready weapons. Others went running back to the room of the master and lifted the senseless body of big Lorenzo.

They found José Rezan breathing, but senseless. He would not be married on the morrow. That much was sure. A driving blow from the fist of the stranger had smashed his nose as though a horse had trampled upon him. His throat was swollen and purple where the grip of Sandy Sweyn had rested for a moment.

They carried him to his bed and cared for him tenderly. In the meantime, the telephone was busy, and the sheriff was speaking again at the other end of the line. He only waited until he heard the name of Sweyn. He dropped his receiver and made for the horse which, day and night, was always saddled, ready to receive him. As he ran down the hall, the door of his daughter's room opened, and he saw her pale, strained face in the glow of the lamplight from her room.

"Dad, it is Sandy Sweyn again?" cried she.

"Aye," said the sheriff, "Sandy Sweyn!"

"He has not killed a man?" cried Peggy Kilmer.

He paused for one startled backward glance at her. Plainly she was in an agony of dread.

"I don't know," muttered the sheriff. "I don't know. I hope not, honey. I'll be back before long."

Then he rushed away through the night. He knew, now, what he had only guessed in the earlier evening. Sandy Sweyn was something more than a mere chance acquaintance to his daughter. It made his heart sore to think of it. He was an honest man, was the sheriff. He may be forgiven if, as he galloped his horse furiously down the valley, he hoped fervently that the mischief which Sandy Sweyn had done this night might be enough to keep him secure behind prison bars until the madness should have died from the brain of Peggy. If, indeed, it would ever die.

He knew her very well, and he knew that, when once her heart was made up, it would not soon be changed.

# 24

When the sheriff arrived, he found six men guarding the bound form of Sandy Sweyn. So far as he could see, there was no sign of any harm done to Sandy himself. His head was high and jaunty, and in the eyes which so many men had called dull there was still burning that brilliant yellow light of life. He greeted the sheriff with a careless and confident smile, and Sheriff Kilmer passed on without saying a word.

He reached the wreckage of the upper hall of the house. He passed on to a room where the two brothers, Vicente and Lorenzo, lay on two beds, silent, controlling their agony with set teeth. He gave them one look, and then went with his guide to the chamber where the master of the house lay, his pale face almost obscured with bandages.

"Something is gone inside of me, sheriff," he said faintly. "He hit me in the face and in the body, when he came at me. The blow in the face broke my nose. The one in the body turned me numb, and I'm still numb, now. That's the window that he came through. My father had it barred with the iron when he had the feud — you remember? — with the sheepherders!"

The sheriff stepped to the window. The bars had been fastened in place with a thick layer of stout cement. That cement was torn away. One bar remained only drawn to the side, instead of being torn bodily away. It was greatly bent, and the sheriff, using all the force in his wiry body, strove to complete the removal of that single bar. He could stir it a little back and forth, but he could not break it out entirely, neither could he bend it any farther back.

A broad-shouldered vaquero stood beside him.

"I have tried it, too," said he in an awed whisper. "But I cannot break it out. Consider, señor, that this devil, climbing up from the outside, could not have had more than one hand free for pulling at the bars!"

Kilmer put his head out and looked down. The wall fell sheer away, a dizzy height, and it seemed to him that there was nothing where a man could plant his feet. He drew back with a little shudder and returned to his prisoner. He examined the ends of Sandy's fingers. One nail was splintered and the very tips of all the other fingers were a little chafed. It was a conclusive proof, to Kilmer. By power of hand alone the stranger had drawn himself up that steep wall, with such deadly peril to life and limb that Kilmer hardly dared to conceive.

Still in silence, Sheriff Kilmer substituted for the many ropes a single pair of stout handcuffs. The prisoner was placed in a buckboard and, with a voluntary guard from among the men of Rezan, he was brought to the jail.

It was a modern jail, built, through the importunities of the sheriff himself, of strong natural stone for walls, with strong steel bars for the block of cells. Into one of these he showed the prisoner.

Kilmer sat down outside the bars and loaded his pipe, and he lighted it carefully.

"Now, Sweyn," he said, "I'd like to know what devil got into you. How did you come to try to murder three men to-night?"

"Three?" asked Sandy mildly. "No, sheriff, only one!"

"Sandy," said the sheriff, a little moved, "I want you to realize that whatever you tell me here will be repeated in the court before the face of the judge and the jury. Do you understand? Whatever you confess to me now will be used against you. Still, I'd really like to know what was in your mind. Because you look rough to me, but you don't look like a midnight murderer! Not you!"

Sandy Sweyn shook his head.

"I never meant to kill three," said he, "but only one. That one it was my right to kill, of course."

"Of course? Of course?" echoed the sheriff. "Man, what gave you a warrant to kill any one?"

Some of the light departed from the eyes of Sandy, and for a moment the sheriff could understand what people meant who had called him a half-wit.

"What warrant?" said Sandy Sweyn. "Why, sheriff, he was to marry Catalina Mirandos tomorrow!"

"What the devil has *that* to do with it?" asked the sheriff.

"Everything," said Sandy, recovering some of his confidence. "Everything, of course, because I am the man who will marry her!"

The sheriff stared. Then he rose and paced up and down the floor of the alley between the cells. Then he came back and took his place on his stool again.

"Go on," said he. "You're to marry little Catalina, then? And does she know about it?"

"I did not speak to her in words. But her eyes said yes, I think!"

"You've seen her, eh?"

"Of course."

"Of course? It's the first that I've heard about it, and I think that if you'd called at the Mirandos house, I *should* have heard. When did you go there?"

"Just before I came to your house for food."

"You saw Señor Mirandos and his daughter — and they didn't let me know that you had been there! This begins to look like a devil of mystery."

"I did not see the señor."

"What? Would the girl see you alone? More mysterious still!"

"I climbed up to the window of her room and went in to speak with her."

"The devil! She didn't call for help?"

"She started to run away, but she changed her mind. We did not talk long, but we said enough, I think!"

The sheriff tilted back his head with a long whistle.

"I'd never believe it!" said he. "And yet — I can't disbelieve you. Anything seems possible to you, young fellow. But after you had talked to Catalina, you decided that you would marry her — and you went singing down the valley?"

"Yes."

"Intending to kill Don José? Don't answer me unless you fully realize that your confession is damned dangerous."

"Of course I intended to kill him."

"Will you tell me why you take it for

granted that you had to kill José?"

"That is something that even a child could understand. I have said that he was to marry the girl to-morrow, and I had to stop that marriage."

"Ten thousand devils! And so you would stop it by killing the man?"

"I could not ask Catalina to break her word to him. You will see that, of course."

The sheriff groaned.

"This is a mess such as no judge in the world ever tried to unravel before!" he said gloomily, shaking his head. "I am glad that *I* don't have to sit on the bench and pass judgment! Man — child — fool — whatever you are, you deliberately decided to kill this Rezan?"

"I did not intend to harm him, at first," said Sandy Sweyn. "All I wanted was to steal Elena Blanca away again. But I thought that I would see this Catalina first, and after I had seen her, I knew that I wanted her more than I wanted Elena. Now, Don José had stolen the mare from me. With that stolen horse, he got the hand of Elena. Also, he tried to keep me from coming to her. He posted four men to keep me from it. The first two tried to kill me with the heat of the sun. They tied me in it."

"The devil they did!"

"It is true, however. And the second two

tried to kill me with their guns."

"I know — I think I know."

"Therefore, certainly it is clear that I have a right to kill José Rezan if I can. He robbed me, and then he tried to murder me!"

The sheriff scratched his head.

"And the other two that you piled up in the room on top of Rezan?"

"I ask you fairly, sheriff. Did they have a right to interfere between me and the man that I had a right to kill?"

It seemed so clear to Sandy Sweyn that he leaned back and smiled in a broad and open confidence at the sheriff. Sheriff Kilmer gasped. Then he stood up.

"Sandy," said he, "maybe I'm violating my oath as the sheriff of this county, but I can't help seeing that you're different from other men. I'm going to forget everything that you've told me. And I'm going to send the best lawyer that I know about to you. Maybe he can do you some good. I don't know of anything else that can! In the meantime, I hope that you sleep well. Adios, Sandy. I'm sorry to see you in this mess. But I've got to tell you this, to begin with:

"A man who breaks into another man's house in the middle of the night, with intent to rob, is a burglar, and as such he stands in danger of taking a mighty long sentence from the judge. The man who breaks into another man's house, in the middle of the night, to commit a murder on him, is going to get about as long a sentence as the law allows — or else be sent for life to some insane asylum. Heaven knows where you'd be better off! Good night, Sandy. I'm sorry for you!"

With that the sheriff turned out into the night. He said first to the jail keeper: "Sam, do you know what we've got in the jail tonight?"

"Sure," said Sam. "We've got that Sweyn, sheriff. The half-wit, of course. I know that."

"No, Sam," said the sheriff, "but I'll tell you the truth. We've got a grizzly bear in there! And, if I were you, I wouldn't trust to any weakness of his wits. If I were you, I'd see to it that every half hour of the night I walked down through that alley between the cells with a shotgun in my hands — that big, double-barreled shotgun, yonder, loaded with the big slugs. Because, you may have to use it. And if you do have to use it, don't shoot for the legs to stop him. Shoot to kill!"

When the sheriff got to his home, he found what he had expected to find. Peggy was waiting for him. He had left his house really interested only in what reaction Peggy would have to this affair. Although a great part of his interest was back yonder in the cell, in the strangest prisoner that had ever fallen into his hands, still his daughter came first by long odds.

He put his horse up, and went around to Peggy's window, and peered into her room. He found her sitting beside a lamp in which the flame was turned down low. There was a book in her lap, but she could not maintain even a pretense of interest in it. Her face was white, and her vacant eyes were turned toward the empty blackness of the window beyond which her father was standing.

Sheriff Kilmer came slowly around to the back door and let himself in. It was as bad as he could have feared, possibly. This odd chap had worked into the secret heart of poor Peggy, and now it was Kilmer's determination to get him out, if he could.

He had barely opened the kitchen door and stepped into the house before he heard the slippered feet of Peggy, as she came running.

"Was there anything wrong, dad?"

He could hardly force himself to look into that strained face.

"When I got to the house of Rezan, I found things in a mess. This Sweyn, that we've seen, had been there. Do you know what he had done?"

Her voice was nothing more than a husky whisper.

"Don't ask me to guess — only tell me, quickly — no dead man?"

"No one dead," said the sheriff, "but just about as bad, I can tell you!"

Peggy had slipped against the wall and leaned there with eyes half closed, breathing slowly and deeply. "Oh, I'm thankful for that!"

Certainly there was no shame in her. She did not care in the least if her father should guess how the stranger had moved her heart. The sheriff was not in a mood for talking about such tender subjects. If it were possible to raise horror in the heart of the girl, he intended to try his hand at it.

"I'll tell you what that man did — not a man, a gorilla — he got to the house of Rezan and climbed up the wall clear to the top story — holding onto the crevices by the tips of his fingers only."

"Aye," said Peggy Kilmer, a faint fire coming to her eyes. "I knew that he could do a thing like that. There's the strength of a giant in him. I could tell that by the first glance."

The sheriff bit his lip.

"There he tore out the iron bars that the old don put up at the time of the feud with the sheep men."

"With his bare hands?"

"His bare hands!"

"Wonderful!"

"Wonderful? Then he swung himself into that room, and I tell you that he dropped to the floor and ran at Don José."

"Was Don José asleep while the bars were being torn from his window?"

"No, he was awake and shooting."

"Ah, good heavens!"

"But Sweyn got him by the throat and —"

"Sandy was not hurt, then!"

"Confound it, Peggy, you really act like an idiot. Have you no sympathy for poor Rezan?"

"Of course — of course. But what happened then?"

"Two more men that Rezan had wisely posted in the hall of his house, came running in and tried to handle this Sweyn. He smashed them almost to bits, and it took the whole household to beat Sweyn down and tie him. I got him then, and put him in the jail. Confound me if the madman doesn't talk as if it were the most natural thing in the world!"

"And wasn't it?" asked the girl.

"What!" cried her father.

"Why, dad, he had tried to have his men destroy —"

"Confound it, Peggy, you talk like — Well, now I have to tell you the rest of the story

— the reason why he really wanted to kill Rezan."

He had hoped that he would not have to use this weapon against her. He had hoped that the picture of Sweyn, like a long-armed gorilla, climbing the wall of the house, and tearing his way in to murder a man, would have been enough to revolt her. Apparently she was not touched.

"It was because the marriage of Don José and little Catalina was set for to-morrow!"

Now he had touched her, to be sure. The color which had been surging back into her cheeks, making her pretty face almost beautiful, now was being swept away again at a stroke.

"Because of that?" murmured Peggy, looking suddenly down at the floor.

"You'll never believe it, Peggy. But this wild man had climbed to the room of Catalina — seen her — gone mad with the love of her —"

Peggy reached for the wall, found it, and steadied herself against it.

"And then?" gasped out poor Peggy.

"Finally the madman decided that the only thing that was left for him to do, was simply to murder this Rezan, so that the girl, if you'll believe me, would not have the trouble of breaking her word to José Rezan! Yes, sir, he considers that Rezan is his by right — and with Rezan dead, he, Sandy Sweyn, will marry the Mexican beauty! Isn't it enough to make you laugh?"

"Yes," said Peggy faintly. "Enough to make one laugh — but — it's pretty late. I'm going to bed!"

She went slowly off toward her room.

The sheriff closed his teeth upon his pipe so hard that the stem splintered in a dozen shards under the pressure.

But he went to bed feeling that he had done a good day's work successfully.

# 25

In the black hour which precedes the rising of the sun, a figure skulked close to the wall of the jail, until it came to the little rear door, set strongly into the wall, and secured by an outward tangle of strong iron bars.

It was Peggy Kilmer. From beneath her cloak she produced now a number of keys, tried two or three and finally fitted one to the lock. It opened easily, noiselessly, for Sheriff Kilmer was not one to allow the locks at his jail to grow rusty. So she drew the door wide, and a whistling gust of wind rushed into the interior of the jail.

Closing the door hastily behind her, she leaned for a moment against the wall, faint with fear, listening to the beating of her heart.

The whistling burst of wind had not caused alarm, apparently, within the jail. There was no sound of voice or footfall. When the silence had continued for a moment, she began a stealthy progress toward the nest of cells.

She had not taken half a dozen steps when a door at the farther side of the big apartment opened suddenly, and a shaft of yellow light struck her full in the face.

Terror made her collapse. She dropped to the floor, and waited, unnerved, for discovery. It did not follow.

Sam carried his lantern into the place for his final tour of inspection, stepping along with a weary stride. The swinging lantern which he carried threw waves of barred shadows up the walls and flooded onto the white ceiling. At the cell of Sandy Sweyn, he paused and held the lantern high.

"Still awake, eh?" said Sam. "Still waiting?"

There was no answer. Peggy, looking through the forest of crossed and intercrossed bars before her, could see the prisoner sitting erect, his arms folded, with a flame in his yellow eyes, as he smiled at the guard.

"Well," said Sam, "in half an hour more there'll be sunrise light, and that's the end of your hopes, young feller. Keep that fact in your mind, will you? And — if I was you, I'd go to sleep. You must be plumb tuckered out."

Sam turned away, and his hobnail shoes gritted upon the concrete floor as he left the room. The heavy door closed with a ponderous sigh behind him and showed, at last, only a thin rim of light outlining the rectangle of the door.

Peggy crept to her feet and hurried softly

to the cell. There was a night-light in the jail — a single smoking lamp — which burned in a far corner, making the cells and the steel bars seem ten times their normal size. By that light, it seemed to the girl that it was a monster rather than a man who was waiting there in the cell.

She had studied the keys before. One was for the door; this for the leg irons. When the irons were loosened, and fell away heavily into her trembling hands, she looked up, and saw the faint glimmer of those yellow eyes above her. Still Sandy had not spoken! She fitted the last key of all into the handcuffs, and now the man was free to do as he pleased.

He did not rise.

"Hurry!" whispered Peggy Kilmer at last. "The irons are off. The door is open. I left my own horse outside, and I think that he'll carry your weight — for a ways. Here's an ammunition belt and a Colt. Don't use it unless you have to, Sandy Sweyn!"

He would not take the proffered weapon, but reached out and took her face between both his hands.

"What'll they be doing to you, Peggy, when they find out that you've turned me loose?"

"I don't know," said Peggy, "and I don't care! They'll never find out, if I can get back quickly enough."

"I got a feeling," said Sandy Sweyn, closing his eyes in intense thought, "that maybe it would be best if I was to stay here and see this thing right through! Better than letting a girl save me from the jail!"

"Don't you understand? It's not a question of fairness. They'll put you in prison for years and years. I've heard my father talk. They'll coop you up in the darkness, Sandy. Maybe they'll never let you out. They can do queer things if they want to!"

"But you see," said Sandy Sweyn earnestly, "I had to do it. I had to try to kill that José Rezan, didn't I? It was the only way, wasn't it?"

"I don't know — I don't know! But hurry, Sandy. Sam may come back any minute! And if he comes — if he comes and finds me here —"

"You're right," said Sandy Sweyn. "If the sheriff wouldn't believe that I'm right and Rezan is wrong, would any judge believe it either?"

"No," said Peggy Kilmer, "no judge would be as easy on you as my dad!"

"I believe you, and I'm going with you, Peggy."

He glided beside her from the jail, and she turned the key in the lock. All seemed blackest night still. Sandy raised his head and took a breath.

"The dawn'll be up in another minute," said he. "D'you smell the morning coming? Aye, there's the rim of it beginning."

It seemed impossible to detect the change. Only, the eastern mountains were a little blacker than the western, and the eastern stars were turning pale, while the western stars still shone bright. It was the faint beginning of the dawn.

"I've got to hurry!" gasped out Peggy Kilmer. "Goodby, Sandy. Take good care of that mustang!"

"I don't need your horse," said Sandy. "My own must be somewhere around here, waiting for me."

"Your own? Waiting for you?"

"Don't tell me that they caught her!"

"Caught her? Not that I know of."

"Then she would follow them along like a dog, when they brought me away from Rezan's house, and she would have stayed just out of sight behind them until she seen them bring me into this place. Then she would stay around and wait, because that's her way! Come over that next hill, and I'll try to call her!"

They crossed the low, wooded ridge, side by side, with the slippery pine needles under their feet, and the pure sweetness of the pine trees in their nostrils.

Where the trees hung like a veil around them, she heard Sandy Sweyn whistling long and shrill, like the whistle of a bird. It did not jar against the ear of the night. It melted into it, and she could only judge of its strength and carrying power by the echo which presently came faintly flying back to them from across the little valley.

In the blackness they waited, and while they stood a rosy pencil streaked the horizon line in the east, just above the hills as they joined the sky. Presently, a distant rhythm was felt rather than heard, and then came the unmistakable noise of a galloping horse.

"It's Cleo," said Sandy Sweyn, with a sigh of relief. "I knew she wouldn't fail to come to me."

Here was the blue roan. She came like a winged thing out from the shadows of the trees and plunged at her master. Now he stood with one arm thrown over her head.

"What I don't make out, though," said Sandy Sweyn, "is how you could do this for me, or why you should do it?"

"A woman doesn't have to have reasons for everything," said Peggy.

"That doesn't go," said Sandy. "I can see through that. I've got one more thing to do, and then I'm coming back to see you. May I come?"

"I can't keep you away; I'm not a whole posse," said Peggy Kilmer, laughing. "But before you go, you'll give me one promise?"

"I'll give you a hundred."

"That you'll not use that gun against another man unless your back is against the wall, Sandy."

"It's a good deal to ask," said Sandy. "What if they hunt me?"

"You can keep away from them if you want to. You know that you can!"

"Tell me this. Is Rezan to marry Catalina tomorrow?"

"No, of course not. He'll spend a week in bed, they say. Or maybe a month! He's badly hurt where you struck him in the body!"

"Then," said Sandy, "I'll promise to do no harm with this gun for a month."

Peggy gasped.

"But you *do* promise, Sandy?"

"On my honor."

"Then — so long."

"So long, Peggy. You'll be late home. The sun is pushing a lot higher."

She realized that as she swung into the saddle on the mustang which she had intended should carry Sandy away to freedom. When she came to the next hill and looked back, there was plenty of light to show her Sandy Sweyn still standing at the side of Cleo. He took off his hat and waved to her. Then she was swinging away on the straight road toward her father's house.

As she galloped the mustang fiercely on, hoping against hope that she might arrive before her father's wakening time, she realized that Sandy Sweyn had given her no thanks for the help which she had brought to him on this night. However, manners were not what one expected from him, or the usual way of doing anything.

In the meantime the east grew rosier and rosier with flooding light. When she came in sight of the house her heart sank, for she saw the smoke rising slowly from the kitchen chimney and sloping in a long, white column across the valley.

She did what one would have expected from Peggy Kilmer. She went straight up to the kitchen door, and there she threw herself from the saddle. The door opened at the same moment, and there stood the sheriff before her.

There was no torrent of questions or guesses or reproaches from his lips. There was merely: "Morning, Peggy. Where the devil is the sharp butcher knife? I can't get the bacon cut with that other infernal thing!"

She brought the sharp butcher knife, and

she sliced the bacon, waiting in a tremor for the trial to begin.

As she poured his coffee and finally sat opposite him at the table, watching him eat, she began to realize that there *would* be no crisis. He simply sat with a pale face, and lips compressed with an iron determination.

By that she could guess how deeply she had cut him. It had been a necessary act from her viewpoint; from his, it was a betrayal!

She endured it until she could stand the pain no longer. Then she stood up and placed the keys on the table.

"He's gone away on the roan mare, dad," she said at last. "I don't know where. I only know — that I wish that I were a man, and a stranger, so that you could treat me the way that I deserve!"

The sheriff did not so much as look up. He kept his glance fixed upon his coffee cup, into which he was stirring the sugar industriously.

# 26

The whole valley learned the news before the morning was an hour older. The sheriff sent the tidings far and wide, sitting at his telephone and ringing number after number.

He talked to the judge first of all. His honor listened to the story with many most illegal curses.

"What's in the girl's idiot head?" asked the judge. "Has she lost her mind about a half-wit, Kilmer?"

"I'm not guessing," said the sheriff sadly. "I'm telling *what* she did, and not why she did it. The question is — what should we do with her? She's broken the law, your honor. She's broken it bad!"

"Leave her be!" said the judge. "When a fool girl gets sentimental there's no use in trying to discipline her back into her senses. No use in the world! Cheer up, Kilmer. This will turn out for the best. By the way, who's laying the charges against Sandy Sweyn? We ought to know that."

"Why, José Rezan, of course — I suppose,"

300

said the sheriff. "I'll get a statement from him at once."

In the meantime, a youngster on a fast horse had brought to the house of Rezan a little pink envelope addressed in the handwriting which meant more than all others to honest José Rezan. He tore it open eagerly. In place of a message of sad and loving condolence, he read within:

José, José, do you know that they are hunting Señor Sweyn up and down the valley to-day? And for what crime? For having attacked you and your men in your own house. Where he, poor simple man, thought that he had a right to go to seek redress after you had robbed him of Elena Blanca. I am told that you are the only person who can lay a charge against Señor Sweyn. I know that that charge will not be pressed. There is too much generosity in you.

Let the boy know when you are well enough to receive a visit from your devoted Catalina.

Poor José read this letter again and again. It made him excessively ill at ease, but there was certainly a shred of justice in what Catalina said.

What shocked him, indeed, was simply the vein of chivalry which appeared to have developed in her at this late moment. Chivalry in Catalina, of all the people in the world!

However, there was not much time remaining to ponder upon this note, for now the sheriff was announced to him. When Kilmer entered, he spoke as though he had just been looking over Rezan's shoulder to read that same letter.

"Rezan," said he, "I want you to swear out a formal warrant before I start rampaging up and down the valley to find this Sandy Sweyn who's made a monkey out of us all!"

"How in the name of all that is wonderful," said Rezan, "could he have escaped? They say that the door to his cell was found unlocked, and the rear door to the jail!"

"How he got away is interesting, but not important," said the sheriff. "What is to the point now, is getting him back. I need a posse to help me with that rascal, and I need your warrant before I open a case against the fellow. Can you write enough to sign your name?"

"Enough to sign it a hundred times," answered José Rezan. "But I'll never write it under a warrant to arrest this Sweyn. And the reason, sheriff, is simply that I got what I more or less deserved. I tried to impose on a poor half-wit, and the poor half-wit that I had robbed turned around and nearly wrecked me and my home!"

"The whole world has gone mad with its talk on the side of Sandy Sweyn. I begin to think that crime pays. It's a moral virtue — to hear you madmen talk about Sandy!"

"Sheriff," said José Rezan, closing his eyes and shaking his bandaged head, "I do not complain. Hunt up another witness. I'll not serve against Sweyn!"

That news spread instantly abroad. The sheriff was not one to allow head hunters to proceed with their work when they did not have law and order behind them. Since the work of law and order had been checked by the odd inconstancy of José Rezan, the sheriff sent out riders to call back his hunters. They came, and they came without tidings of the hunted. One thought that he had seen a blue roan shadow moving through the trees here; another thought that he had seen a bluish horse galloping down a hollow — but all was on the testimony of fleeting glimpses of which they could not be sure. So it was that Sandy Sweyn went unscathed after such a career of wildness as the valley had never seen before.

As that day wore toward a close, a dozen armed men guarded every inch of the ground around José Rezan's house. Around the corral where Elena Blanca was kept, Señor Mirandos had posted more warriors. It was commonly felt that if the wild man chose to strike again, it would be in one of the two places, although Mirandos was rather startled by a telephone message from the sheriff, saying: "While you're on your guard, keep an eye on your daughter to-night, Mirandos."

"A thousand thanks," said Mirandos.

When he hung up the telephone he smiled to himself. The rest of the world might regard his Catalina as a shrinking flower and a tender bud, but he, who knew her for these many years, felt that she was the last person in the world to need any cherishing from any person, even from her father. He paid no heed to establishing any guard over his daughter.

Little Catalina was left strictly alone. She had spent the entire day in her room. She was smiling and gay in the morning when she heard of the escape of the prisoner. But as the day wore on the miracle which she had expected did not develop. No Sandy Sweyn came to her, and toward night she grew into a towering passion.

Something had to bear the brunt of it when nine in the evening came and no wild lover appeared at either window. When poor Dick stood up and stretched himself with a yawn she flew into a mad, unreasoning passion, snatched up a whip, cut him twice with it, and as he fled with a howl, she threw the whip after him and stamped with all the passion in her furious little body.

Poor Dick! He would never know that in this moment he had accomplished his destiny and one more good service to the world than any other of his kind in many and many a year. At that moment, as the whip was raised and cut against his tender hide, a shadowy head had risen at the casement of the bedroom. Two blazing, yellow eyes watched the scene, then the head slowly disappeared.

Catalina rushed into her inner chamber to be utterly alone with her disappointment, but Dick, cowering in the corner, suddenly came to life and hurried toward the casement, whining softly.

To another girl that evening brought no eager expectations. Peggy Kilmer felt that she had abdicated in behalf of her rival. There was not the slightest doubt in her mind that Sandy Sweyn was mad with love of Catalina. How could Peggy guess that a dog, a mere dog, might come between?

In the soft black of the night, Peggy sat in the hammock outside the sheriff's house and watched the stars which shimmered through the trees above her. She stroked old Tabby, who lay purring in her lap. Purring in her lap one minute, but with a snarl and a gasp here was Tabby scooting up the trunk of the first tree and spitting from the branches, while a dog whined underneath, eager-eyed.

"Heavens above!" said Peggy Kilmer. "It's Dick — it's Catalina's dog!"

We will sometimes speak our thoughts aloud, when we feel ourselves most securely alone, and Peggy spoke hers aloud on this night. A deep voice answered her at once from the thick of the black night beneath the tree.

"Aye, it's Catalina's dog. I went looking for a girl, and I only came away with a dog. Sit down here, Peggy. I'm gunna tell you why."

Sit down by the side of a stranger like Sandy Sweyn? She had not time or chance to make up her own mind. For Sandy scooped her lightly into the hollow of his arm, and there they sat in the hammock, side by side.

"I went up the valley to the Mirandos house," said Sandy, "looking to find Catalina, because that pretty face of hers has been living here behind my eyes for the last day, you understand?"

"I understand," said Peggy faintly.

"When I got there, I worked my way up to her window, as I'd done before, and as I got there, I was just in time to see her take a whip and flog this dog — flog him for nothing at all. Why, Peggy, when I watched it,

306

it turned things into a red blur. I wanted to take her by the throat. I waited till she was out of the room, and then I scooped up Dick and brought him down here. What I want to know is, do you think that a delicate dog like this could follow me the way I live, in the woods, without getting sick?"

"I think he could — I know he could!" said Peggy with more animation.

"Well," said Sandy Sweyn, "you think you would trust a dog to me, then?"

"I would, Sandy."

"Then there's one thing more, Peg. There were two faces in my mind. One very pretty, and one very freckled. One of them has gone out, to-night, and I'll never see it again. That leaves the freckled one, Peg. And that leaves one question more that I've got to ask. If you'd trust a dog to me, Peg, d'you think that one day you would trust yourself?"

"I —" gasped out Peggy. "I — How can I tell?"

"Who but you could?"

"Dad, and he's yonder in the house."

"The sheriff!" cried Sandy Sweyn.

"Aye," said Peggy with a strange note in her voice, "and I think that he's sort of expecting you to call!"

"I'll do it," said Sandy Sweyn. "The sheriff is a fair man, and I'll do it. Dick, you come along and back me up!"

He started slowly toward the lighted window of the house, with the setter close against his heels.

**Max Brand** is the best-known pen name of Frederick Faust, creator of Dr. Kildare, Destry, and many other fictional characters popular with readers and viewers worldwide. Faust wrote for a variety of audiences in many genres. His enormous output, totaling approximately thirty million words or the equivalent of 530 ordinary books, covered nearly every field: crime, fantasy, historical romance, espionage, Westerns, science fiction, adventure, animal stories, love, war, and fashionable society, big business and big medicine. Eighty motion pictures have been based on his work along with many radio and television programs. For good measure he also published four volumes of poetry. Perhaps no other author has reached more people in more different ways.

Born in Seattle in 1892, orphaned early, Faust grew up in the rural San Joaquin Valley of California. At Berkeley he became a student rebel and one-man literary movement, contributing prodigiously to all campus publications. Denied a degree because of unconventional conduct, he embarked on a series of adventures culminating in New York City where, after a period of near starvation, he recieved simultaneous recognition as a serious poet and successful popular-prose writer. Later, he traveled widely, making his home in New York, then in Florence, and finally in Los Angeles.

Once the United States entered the Second World War, Faust abandoned his lucrative writing career and his work as a screenwriter to serve as a war correspondent with the infantry in Italy, despite his fifty-one years and a bad heart. He was killed during a night attack on a hilltop village held by the German army. New books based on magazine seriels or unpublished manuscripts continue to appear. Alive and dead he has averaged a new one every four months for seventy-five years. In the U.S. alone nine publishers issue his work, plus many foreign countries. Yet, only recently have the full dimensions of this extraordinarily versatile and prolific writer come to be recognized and his stature as a protean literary figure in the 20th Century acknowledged. His popularity continues to grow throughout the world.